Beyond the Gates

Elizabeth Stuart Phelps

Alpha Editions

This edition published in 2021

ISBN : 9789354844607

Design and Setting By
Alpha Editions
www.alphaedis.com
Email - info@alphaedis.com

As per information held with us this book is in Public Domain.
This book is a reproduction of an important historical work. Alpha Editions
uses the best technology to reproduce historical work in the same manner
it was first published to preserve its original nature. Any marks or number
seen are left intentionally to preserve its true form.

BEYOND THE GATES.

I.

I HAD been ill for several weeks with what they called brain fever. The events which I am about to relate happened on the fifteenth day of my illness.

Before beginning to tell my story, it may not be out of place to say a few words about myself, in order to clarify to the imagination of the reader points which would otherwise involve numerous explanatory digressions, more than commonly misplaced in a tale dealing with the materials of this.

I am a woman forty years of age. My father was a clergyman; he had been many years dead. I was living, at the time I refer to, in my mother's house in a factory town in Massachusetts. The town need not be more particularly mentioned, nor genuine family names given, for obvious reasons. I was the oldest of four children; one of my sisters was married, one was at home with us, and there was a boy at college.

I was an unmarried, but not an unhappy woman. I had reached a very busy, and sometimes I hoped a not altogether valueless, middle age. I had used life and loved it. Beyond the idle impulse of a weary moment, which signifies no more than the reflex action of a mental muscle, and which I had been in the habit of rating accordingly, I had never wished to die. I was well, vigorous, and active. I was not of a dependent or a despondent temperament.

I am not writing an autobiography, and these things, not of importance in themselves, require only the briefest allusion. They will serve to explain the general cast of my life, which in turn may define the features of my story.

There are two kinds of solitary: he who is drawn by the inward, and he who chooses the outward life. To this latter class I had belonged. Circumstances, which it is not necessary to detail here, had thrust me into the one as a means of self-preservation from the other, while I was yet quite young.

I had been occupied more largely with the experiences of other people than with my own. I had been in the habit of being depended upon. It had been my great good fortune to be able to spend a part of my time among the sick, the miserable, and the poor. It had been, perhaps, my better chance to be obliged to balance the emotional perils of such occupations by those of a different character. My business was that of a school-teacher, but I had traveled somewhat; I had served as a nurse during the latter years of the war; in the Sanitary Commission; upon the Freedmen's Bureau; as an officer in a Woman's Prison, and had done a little work for the State Bureau of Labor among the factory operatives of our own town. I had therefore, it will be seen, been spared the deterioration of a monotonous existence. At the time I was taken ill I was managing a private school, rather large for the corps of assistants which I could command, and had overworked. I had been at home, thus employed, with my mother who needed me, for two years.

It may not be unsuitable, before proceeding with my narrative, to say that I had been a believer in the truths of the Christian religion; not, however, a devotee. I had not the ecstatic temperament, and was not known among my friends for any higher order of piety than that which is implied in trying to do one's duty for Christ's sake, and saying little about it or Him,—less than I wish I had sometimes. It was natural to me to speak in other ways than by words; that does not prove that it was best. I had read a little, like all thinking people with any intellectual margin to their lives, of the religious controversies of the day, and had not been without my share of pressure from the fashionable reluctance to believe. Possibly this had affected a temperament not too much inclined towards the supernatural, but it had never conquered my faith, which I think had grown to be dearer to me because I had not kept it without a fight for it. It certainly had become, for this reason, of greater practical value. It certainly had become, for this and every reason, the most valuable thing I had, or hoped to have. I believed in God and immortality, and in the history of Jesus Christ. I respected and practiced prayer, but chiefly decided what I ought to do next minute. I loved life and lived it. I neither feared death nor thought much about it.

When I had been ill a fortnight, it occurred to me that I was very sick, but not that I could possibly die. I suffered a good deal at first; after that much less. There was great misery for lack of sleep, and intolerable restlessness. The worst, however, was the continuity of care. Those who have borne heavy responsibilities for any length of time will understand me. The incessant burden pressed on: now a pupil had fallen into some disgraceful escapade; now the investments of my mother's, of which I had the charge, had failed on the dividends; then I had no remittance for the boy at college; then my sister, in a heart-breaking emergency, confided to me a peril against which I could not lift a finger; the Governor held me responsible for the typhoid among the prisoners; I added eternal columns of statistics for the Charity Boards, and found forever a mistake in each report; a dying soldier called to me in piercing tones for a cup of water; the black girl to whom I read the Gospel of John, drowned her baby; I ran six looms in the mill for the mother of six children till her seventh should be born; I staked the salvation of my soul upon answering the argument of Strauss to the satisfaction of an unbelieving friend, and lost my wager; I heard my classes in Logic, and was unable to repeat anything but the "Walrus and the Carpenter," for the "Barbara Celarent." Suddenly, one day, in the thick of this brain-battle, I slipped upon a pause, in which I distinctly heard a low voice say,

"But Thine eternal thoughts move on,
Thine undisturbed affairs."

It was my mother's voice. I perceived then that she sat at my bedside in the red easy-chair, repeating hymns, poor soul! in the hope of calming me.

I put out my hand and patted her arm, but it did not occur to me to speak till I saw that there were masses of pansies and some mignonette upon the table, and I asked who sent them, and she told me the school-girls had kept them fresh there every day since I was taken ill. I felt some pleasure that they should take the trouble to select the flowers I preferred. Then I asked her where the jelly came from, and the grapes, and about other trifles that I saw, such as accumulate in any sick-room. Then she gave me the names of different friends and neighbors who had been so good as to remember me. Chiefly I was touched by the sight of a straggly magenta geranium which I noticed growing in a pot by the window, and which a poor woman from the mills had brought the day before. I asked my mother if there were any letters, and she said, many, but that I must not hear them read; she spoke of some from the prison. The door-bell often rang softly, and I asked why it was muffled, and who called. Alice had come in, and said something in an undertone to mother about the Grand Army and resolutions and sympathy; and she used the names of different people I had almost forgotten, and this confused me. They stopped talking, and I became at once very ill again.

The next point which I recall is turning to see that the doctor was in the room. I was in great suffering, and he gave me a few spoonfuls of something which he said would secure sleep. I desired to ask him what it was, as I objected to narcotics, and preferred to bear whatever was before me with the eyes of my mind open, but as soon as I tried to speak I forgot what I wished to say.

I do not know how long it was before the truth approached me, but it was towards evening of that day, the fifteenth, as I say, of my illness, that I said aloud:

"Mother, Tom is in the room. Why has Tom come home?"

Tom was my little brother at college. He came towards the bed as I spoke. He had his hat in his hand, and he put it up before his eyes.

"Mother!" I repeated louder than before. "*Why have you sent for Tom?*"

But Mother did not answer me. She leaned over me. I saw her looking down. She had the look that she had when my father died; though I was so young when that happened, I had never forgotten my mother's look; and I had never seen it since, from that day until this hour.

"Mother! am I so sick as *that*? MOTHER!"

"Oh, my dear!" cried Mother. "Oh my dear, my dear!" ...

So after that I understood. I was greatly startled that they should feel me to be dangerously ill; but I was not alarmed.

"It is nonsense," I said, after I had thought about it a little while. "Dr. Shadow was always a croaker. I have no idea of dying! I have nursed too many sicker people than I am. I don't *intend* to die! I am able to sit up now, if I want to. Let me try."

"I'll hold you," said Tom, softly enough. This pleased me. He lifted all the pillows, and held me straight out upon his mighty arms. Tom was a great athlete—took the prizes at the gymnasium. No weaker man could have supported me for fifteen minutes in the strained position by which he found that he could give me comfort and so gratify my whim. Tom held me a long time; I think it must have been an hour; but I began to suffer again, and could not judge of time. I wondered how that big boy got such infinite tenderness into those iron muscles. I felt a great respect for human flesh and bone and blood, and for the power and preciousness of the living human body. It seemed much more real to me, then, than the spirit. It seemed an absurdity that any one should suppose that I was in danger of being done with life. I said:—

"I'm going to live, Tom! Tell Mother I have no idea of dying. I prefer to live."

Tom nodded; he did not speak; I felt a hot dash of tears on my face, which surprised me; I had not seen Tom cry since he lost the football match when he was eleven years old.

They gave me something more out of the spoon, again, I think, at that moment, and I felt better. I said to Tom:—

"You see!" and bade them send Mother to lie down, and asked Alice to make her beef-tea, and to be sure and make it as we did in the army. I do not remember saying anything more after this. I certainly did not suffer any more. I felt quiet and assured. Nothing farther troubled me. The room became so still that I thought they must all have gone away, and left me with the nurse, and that she, finding me so well, had herself fallen asleep. This rested me—to feel that I was no longer causing them pain—more than anything could have done; and I began to think the best thing I could do would be to take a nap myself.

With this conviction quietly in mind I turned over, with my face towards the wall, to go to sleep. I grew calmer, and yet more calm, as I lay there. There was a cross of Swiss carving on the wall, hanging over a picture of my father. Leonardo's Christ—the one from the drawing for the Last Supper, that we all know—hung above both these. Owing to my position, I could not see the other pictures in the room, which was large, and filled with little things, the gifts of those who had been kind to me in a life of many busy years. Only these three objects—the cross, the Christ, and my father—came within range of my eyes as the power of sleep advanced. The room was darkened, as it had been since I became so ill, so that I was not sure whether it were night or day. The clock was striking. I think it struck two; and I perceived the odor of the mignonette. I think it was the last thing I noticed before going to sleep, and I remembered, as I did so, the theories which gave to the sense of smell greater significance than any of the rest; and remembered to have read that it was either the last or the first to give way in the dying. (I could not recall, in my confused condition, which.) I thought of this with pleased and idle interest; but did not associate the thought with the alarm felt by my friends about my condition.

I could have slept but a short time when I woke, feeling much easier. The cross, the Christ, and the picture of my father looked at me calmly from the wall on which the sick-lamp cast a steady, soft light. Then I remembered that it was night, of course, and felt chagrined that I could have been confused on this point.

The room seemed close to me, and I turned over to ask for more air.

As I did so, I saw some one sitting in the cushioned window-seat by the open window—the eastern window. No one had occupied this seat, on account of the draught and chill, since my illness. As I looked steadily, I saw that the person who sat there was my father.

His face was turned away, but his figure and the contour of his noble head were not to be mistaken. Although I was a mere girl when he died, I felt no hesitation about this. I knew at once, and beyond all doubt, that it was he. I experienced pleasure, but little, if any, surprise.

As I lay there looking at him, he turned and regarded me. His deep eyes glowed with a soft, calm light; but yet, I know not why, they expressed more love than I had ever seen in them before. He used to love us nervously and passionately. He had now the look of one whose whole nature is saturated with rest, and to whom the fitfulness, distrust, or distress of intense feeling acting upon a super-sensitive organization, were impossible. As he looked towards me, he smiled. He had one of the sweetest smiles that ever illuminated a mortal face.

"Why, Father!" I said aloud. He nodded encouragingly, but did not speak.

"Father?" I repeated, "Father, is this *you*?" He laughed a little, softly, putting up one hand and tossing his hair off from his forehead—an old way of his.

"What are you here for?" I asked again. "Did Mother send for *you*, too?"

When I had said this, I felt confused and troubled; for though I did not remember that he was dead—I mean I did not put the thought in any such form to myself, or use that word or any of its synonyms—yet I remembered that he had been absent from our family circle for a good while, and that if Mother had sent for him because I had a brain fever, it would have been for some reason not according to her habit.

"It is strange," I said. "It isn't like her. I don't understand the thing at all."

Now, as I continued to look at the corner of the room where my father was sitting, I saw that he had risen from the cushioned window-seat, and taken a step or two towards me. He stopped, however, and stood quite still, and looked at me most lovingly and longingly; and *then* it was that he held out his arms to me.

"Oh," cried I, "I wish I could come! But you don't know how sick I am. I have not walked a step for over two weeks."

He did not speak even yet, but still held out his arms with that look of unutterably restful love. I felt the elemental tie between parent and child draw me. It seemed to me as if I had reached the foundation of all human feeling; as if I had gone down—how shall I say it?—below the depths of all other love. I had always known I loved him, but not like that. I was greatly moved.

"But you don't understand me," I repeated with some agitation. "I *can't* walk." I thought it very strange that he did not, in consideration of my feebleness, come to me.

Then for the first time he spoke.

"Come," he said gently. His voice sounded quite natural; I only noticed that he spoke under his breath, as if not to awake the nurse, or any person who was in the room.

At this, I moved, and sat up on the edge of my bed; although I did so easily enough, I lost courage at that point. It seemed impossible to go farther. I felt a little chilly, and remembered, too, that I was not dressed. A warm white woolen wrapper of my own, and my slippers, were within reach, by the head of the bed; Alice wore them when she watched with me. I put these things on, and then paused, expecting to be overcome with exhaustion after the effort. To my surprise, I did not feel tired at all. I believe, rather, I felt a little stronger. As I put the clothes on, I noticed the magenta geranium across the room. These, I think, were the only things which attracted my attention.

"Come here to me," repeated Father; he spoke more decidedly, this time with a touch of authority. I remembered hearing him speak just so when Tom was learning to walk; he began by saying, "Come, sonny boy!" but when the baby played the coward, he said, "My son, come here!"

As if I had been a baby, I obeyed. I put my feet to the floor, and found that I stood strongly. I experienced a slight giddiness for a moment, but when this passed, my head felt clearer than before. I walked steadily out into the middle of the room. Each step was firmer than the other. As I advanced, he came to meet me. My heart throbbed. I thought I should have fallen, not from weakness, but from joy.

"Don't be afraid," he said encouragingly; "that is right. You are doing finely. Only a few steps more. There!"

It was done. I had crossed the distance which separated us, and my dear Father, after all those years, took me, as he used to do, into his arms....

He was the first to speak, and he said:—

"You poor little girl!—But it is over now."

"Yes, it is over now," I answered. I thought he referred to the difficult walk across the room, and to my long illness, now so happily at an end. He smiled and patted me on the cheek, but made no other answer.

"I must tell Mother that you are here," I said presently. I had not looked behind me or about me. Since the first sight of my father sitting in the window, I had not observed any other person, and could not have told who was in the room.

"Not yet," my father said. "We may not speak to her at present. I think we had better go."

I lifted my face to say, "Go where?" but my lips did not form the question. It was just as it used to be when he came from the study and held out his hand, and said "Come," and I went anywhere with him, neither asking, nor caring, so long as it was with him; and then he used to play or walk with me, and I forgot the whole world besides. I put my hand in his without a question, and we moved towards the door.

"I suppose *you* had better go this way," he said, with a slight hesitation, as we passed out and across the hall.

"Any way you like best," I said joyfully. He smiled, and still keeping my hand, led me down the stairs. As we went down, I heard the little Swiss clock, above in my room, strike the half hour after two.

I noticed everything in the hall as we descended; it was as if my vision, as well as the muscles of motion, grew stronger with each moment. I saw the stair-carpeting with its faded Brussels pattern, once rich, and remembered counting the red roses on it the night I went up with the fever on me; reeling and half delirious, wondering how I could possibly afford to be sick. I saw the hat-tree with Tom's coat, and Alice's blue Shetland shawl across the old hair-cloth sofa. As we opened the door, I saw the muffled bell. I stood for a moment upon the threshold of my old home, not afraid but perplexed.

My father seemed to understand my thoughts perfectly, though I had not spoken, and he paused for my reluctant mood. I thought of all the years I had spent there. I thought of my childhood and girlhood; of the tempestuous periods of life which that quiet roof had hidden; of the calms upon which it had brooded. I thought of sorrows that I had forgotten, and those which I had prayed in vain to forget. I thought of temptations and of mistakes and of sins, from which I had fled back asking these four walls to shelter me. I thought of the comfort and blessedness that I had never failed to find in the old house. I shrank from leaving it. It seemed like leaving my body.

When the door had been opened, the night air rushed in. I could see the stars, and knew, rather than felt, that it was cold. As we stood waiting, an icicle dropped from the eaves, and fell, breaking into a dozen diamond flashes at our feet. Beyond, it was dark.

"It seems to me a great exposure," I said reluctantly, "to be taken out into a winter night,—at such an hour, too! I have been so very sick."

"Are you cold?" asked my father gently. After some thought I said:—

"No, sir."

For I was not cold. For the first time I wondered why.

"Are you tired?"

No, I was not tired.

"Are you afraid?"

"A little, I think, sir."

"Would you like to go back, Molly, and rest awhile?"

"If you please, Papa."

The old baby-word came instinctively in answer to the baby-name. He led me like a child, and like a child I submitted. It was like him to be so thoughtful of my weakness. My dear father was always one of those rare men who think of little things largely, and so bring, especially into the lives of women, the daily comfort which makes the infinite preciousness of life.

We went into the parlor and sat down. It was warm there and pleasant. The furnace was well on, and embers still in the grate. The lamps were not lighted, yet the room was not dark. I enjoyed being down there again after all those weeks up-stairs, and was happy in looking at the familiar things, the afghan on the sofa, and the magazines on the table, uncut because of my illness; Mother's work-basket, and Alice's music folded away.

"It was always a dear old room," said Father, seating himself in his own chair, which we had kept for twenty years in its old place. He put his head back, and gazed peacefully about.

When I felt rested, and better, I asked him if we should start now.

"Just as you please," he said quietly. "There is no hurry. We are never hurried."

"If we have anything to do," I said, "I had rather do it now I think."

"Very well," said Father, "that is like you." He rose and held out his hand again. I took it once more, and once more we went out to the threshold of our old home. This time I felt more confidence, but when the night air swept in, I could not help shrinking a little in spite of myself, and showing the agitation which overtook me.

"Father!" I cried, "Father! *where* are we going?"

My father turned at this, and looked at me solemnly. His face seemed to shine and glow. He looked from what I felt was a great height. He said:—

"Are you really afraid, Mary, to go *any*where with me?"

"No, no!" I protested in a passion of regret and trust, "my dear father! I would go any where in earth or Heaven with you!"

"Then come," he said softly.

I clasped both hands, interlocking them through his arm, and we shut the door and went down the steps together and out into the winter dawn.

II.

It was neither dark nor day; and as we stepped into the village streets the confused light trembled about us delicately. The stars were still shining. Snow was on the ground; and I think it had freshly fallen in the night, for I noticed that the way before us lay quite white and untrodden. I looked back over my shoulders as my father closed the gate, which he did without noise. I meant to take a gaze at the old house, from which, with a thrill at the heart, I began to feel that I was parting under strange and solemn conditions. But when I glanced up the path which we had taken, my attention was directed altogether from the house, and from the slight sadness of the thought I had about it.

The circumstance which arrested me was this. Neither my father's foot nor mine had left any print upon the walk. From the front door to the street, the fine fair snow lay unbroken; it stirred, and rose in restless flakes like winged creatures under the gentle wind, flew a little way, and fell again, covering the surface of the long white path with a foam so light, it seemed as if thought itself could not have passed upon it without impression. I can hardly say why I did not call my father's attention to this fact.

As we walked down the road the dawn began to deepen. The stars paled slowly. The intense blue-black and purple of the night sky gave way to the warm grays that precede sunrise in our climate. I saw that the gold and the rose were coming. It promised to be a mild morning, warmer than for several days. The deadly chill was out of the air. The snow yielded on the outlines of the drifts, and relaxed as one looked at it, as snow does before melting, and the icicles had an air of expectation, as if they hastened to surrender to the annunciation of a warm and impatient winter's day.

"It is going to thaw," I said aloud.

"It seems so to you," replied my father, vaguely.

"But at least it is very pleasant," I insisted.

"I'm glad you find it so," he said; "I should have been disappointed if it had struck you as cold, or—gloomy—in any way."

It was still so early that all the village was asleep. The blinds and curtains of the houses were drawn and the doors yet locked. None of our neighbors were astir, nor were there any signs of traffic yet in the little shops. The great factory-bell, which woke the operatives at half-past four, had rung, but this was the only evidence as yet of human life or motion. It did not occur to me, till afterwards, to wonder at the inconsistency between the hour struck by my own Swiss clock and the factory time.

I was more interested in another matter which just then presented itself to me.

The village, as I say, was still asleep. Once I heard the distant hoofs of a horse sent clattering after the doctor, and ridden by a messenger from a household in mortal need. Up to this time we two had seemed to be the only watchers in all the world.

Now, as I turned to see if I could discover whose horse it was and so who was in emergency, I observed suddenly that the sidewalk was full of people. I say full of people; I mean that there was a group behind us; a few, also, before us; some, too, were crossing the street. They conversed together standing at the corners, or walked in twos, as father and I were doing; or strolled, some of them alone. Some of them seemed to have immediate business and to be in haste; others sauntered as he who has no occupation. Some talked and gesticulated earnestly, or laughed loudly. Others went with a thoughtful manner, speaking not at all.

As I watched them I began to recognize here and there, a man, or a woman;—there were more men than women among them, and there were no children.

A few of these people, I soon saw, were old neighbors of ours; some I had known when I was a child, and had forgotten till this moment. Several of them bowed to us as we passed along. One man stopped and waited for us, and spoke to Father, who shook hands with him; intimating, however, pleasantly enough, that he was in haste, and must be excused for passing on.

"Yes, yes, I see," said the man with a glance at me. I then distinctly saw this person's face, and knew him beyond a doubt, for an old neighbor, a certain Mr. Snarl, a miserly, sanctimonious man—I had never liked him.

"Father!" I stopped short. "Father, that man is dead. He has been dead for twenty years!"

Now, at this, I began to tremble; yet not from fear, I think; from amazement, rather, and the great confusion which I felt.

"And there"—I pointed to a pale young man who had been thrown from his carriage (it was said because he was in no condition to drive)—"there is Bobby Bend. He died last winter."

"Well," said Father quietly, "and what then?"

"And over there—why, certainly that is Mrs. Mersey!"

I had known Mrs. Mersey for a lovely woman. She died of a fever contracted in the care of a poor, neglected creature. I saw her at this moment across and far down the street, coming from a house where there was trouble.

She came with a swift, elastic motion, unlike that of any of the others who were about us; the difference was marked, and yet one which I should have found it at that time impossible to describe. Perhaps I might have said that she hovered above rather than touched the earth; but this would not have defined the distinction. As I looked after her she disappeared; in what direction I could not tell.

"So they *are* dead people," I said, with a sort of triumph; almost as if I had dared my father to deny it. He smiled.

"Father, I begin to be perplexed. I have heard of these hallucinations, of course, and read the authenticated stories, but I never supposed I could be a subject of such illusions. It must be because I have been so sick."

"Partly because you have been so sick—yes," said Father drawing down the corners of his mouth, in that way he had when he was amused. I went on to tell him that it seemed natural to see him, but that I was surprised to meet those others who had left us, and that I did not find it altogether agreeable.

"Are you afraid?" he asked me, as he had before. No, I could not say that I was afraid.

"Then hasten on," he said in a different tone, "our business is not with them, at present. See! we have already left them behind."

And, indeed, when I glanced back, I saw that we had. We, too, were now traveling alone together, and at a much faster speed, towards the outskirts of the town. We were moving eastward. Before us the splendid day was coming up. The sky was unfolding, shade above shade, paler at the edge, and glowing at the heart, like the petals of a great rose.

The snow was melting on the moors towards which we bent our steps; the water stood here and there in pools, and glistened. A little winter bird—some chickadee or wood-pecker—was bathing in one of these pools; his tiny brown body glowed in the brightness, flashing to and fro. He chirped and twittered and seemed bursting with joy. As we approached the moors, the stalks of the sumachs, the mulberries, the golden-rod, and asters, all the wayside weeds and the brown things that we never know and never love till winter, rose beautiful from the snow; the icicles melted and dripped from them; the dead-gold-colored leaves of the low oaks rustled; at a distance we heard the sweet sough from a grove of pines; behind us the morning bells of the village broke into bubbles of cheerful sound. As we walked on together I felt myself become stronger at every step; my heart grew light.

"It is a good world," I cried, "it is a good world!"

"So it is," said my father heartily, "and yet—my dear daughter"—He hesitated; so long that I looked into his face earnestly, and then I saw that a strange gravity had settled upon it. It was not like any look that I had ever seen there before.

"I have better things to show you," he said gently.

"I do not understand you, sir."

"We have only begun our journey, Mary; and—if you do not understand—but I thought you would have done so by this time—I wonder if she *is* going to be frightened after all!"

We were now well out upon the moors, alone together, on the side of the hill. The town looked far behind us and insignificant. The earth dwindled and the sky grew, as we looked from one to the other. It seemed to me that I had never before noticed how small a portion of our range of vision is filled by the surface of earth, and what occupies it; and how immense the proportion of the heavens. As we stood there, it seemed to overwhelm us.

"Rise," said my father in a voice of solemn authority, "rise quickly!"

I struggled at his words, for he seemed to slip from me, and I feared to lose him. I struggled and struck out into the air; I felt a wild excitement, like one plunged into a deep sea, and desperately swimming, as animals do, and a few men, from blind instinct, having never learned. My father spoke encouragingly, and with tenderness. He never once let go my hand. I felt myself, beyond all doubt, soaring—slowly and weakly—but surely ascending above the solid ground.

"See! there is nothing to fear," he said from time to time. I did not answer. My heart beat fast. I exerted all my strength and took a stronger stroke. I felt that I gained upon myself. I closed my eyes, looking neither above nor below.

Suddenly, as gently as the opening of a water lily, and yet as swiftly as the cleaving of the lightning, there came to me a thought which made my brain whirl, and I cried aloud:

"Father, *am I* DEAD?" My hands slipped—I grew dizzy—wavered—and fluttered. I was sure that I should fall. At that instant I was caught with the iron of tenderness and held, like a very young child, in my father's arms. He said nothing, only patted me on the cheek, as we ascended, he seeing, and I blind; he strength, and I weakness; he who knew all, and I who knew nothing, silently with the rising sun athwart the rose-lit air.

I was awed, more than there are words to say; but I felt no more fear than I used to do when he carried me on his shoulder up the garden walk, after it grew dark, when I was tired out with play.

III.

I USE the words "ascension" and "arising" in the superficial sense of earthly imagery. Of course, carefully speaking, there can be no up or down to the motion of beings detached from a revolving globe, and set adrift in space. I thought of this in the first moment, with the keenness which distinguishes between knowledge and experience. I knew when our journey came to an end, by the gradual cessation of our rapid motion; but at first I did not incline to investigate beyond this fact. Whether I was only tired, or giddy, or whether a little of what we used to call faintness overcame me, I can hardly say. If this were so, it was rather a spiritual than a physical disability; it was a faintness of the soul. Now I found this more energetic than the bodily sensations I had known. I scarcely sought to wrestle against it, but lay quite still, where we had come to a halt.

I wish to say here, that if you ask me where this was, I must answer that I do not know. I must say distinctly that, though after the act of dying I departed from the surface of the earth, and reached the confines of a different locality, I cannot yet instruct another *where* this place may be.

My impression that it was not a vast distance (measured, I mean, by an astronomical scale) from our globe, is a strong one, which, however, I cannot satisfactorily defend. There seemed to be flowers about me; I wondered what they were, but lay with my face hidden in my arm, not caring yet to look about. I thought of that old-fashioned allegory called "The Distant Hills," where the good girl, when she died, sank upon a bed of violets; but the bad girl slipped upon rolling stones beneath a tottering ruin. This trifling memory occupied me for some moments; yet it had so great significance to me, that I recall it, even now, with pungent gratitude.

"I shall remember what I have read." This was my first thought in the new state to which I had come. Minna was the name of the girl in the allegory. The illustrations were very poor, but had that uncanny fascination which haunts allegorical pictures—often the more powerful because of their rudeness.

As I lay there, still not caring, or even not daring to look up, the fact that I was crushing flowers beneath me became more apparent; a delicate perfume arose and surrounded me; it was like and yet unlike any that I had ever known; its familiarity entranced, its novelty allured me. Suddenly I perceived what it was—

"Mignonette!"

I laughed at my own dullness in detecting it, and could not help wondering whether it were accident or design that had given me for my first experience in the new life, the gratification of a little personal taste like this. For a few moments I yielded to the pure and exquisite perfume, which stole into my whole nature, or it seemed to me so then. Afterwards I learned how little I knew of my "whole nature" at that time.

Presently I took courage, and lifted my head. I hardly know what I expected to see. Visions of the Golden City in the Apocalypse had flitted before me. I thought of the River of Death in the "Pilgrim's Progress," of the last scene in the "Voyage of Life," of Theremin's "Awakening," of several famous books and pictures which I had read or seen, describing what we call Heaven. These works of the human imagination—stored away perhaps in the frontal lobes of the brain, as scientists used to tell us—had influenced my anticipations more than I could have believed possible till that moment.

I was indeed in a beautiful place; but it did not look, in any respect, as I had expected. No; I think not in any respect. Many things which happened to me later, I can describe more vividly than I can this first impression. In one way it was a complex, in another, a marvelously simple one. Chiefly, I think I had a consciousness of safety—infinite safety. All my soul drew a long breath—"Nothing more can happen to me!" Yet, at the same time, I felt that I was at the outset of all experience. It was as if my heart cried aloud, "Where shall I begin?"

I looked about and abroad. My father stood at a little distance from me, conversing with some friends. I did not know them. They had great brightness and beauty of appearance. So, also, had he. He had altered perceptibly since he met me in the lower world, and seemed to glow and become absorbent of light from some source yet unseen. This struck me forcibly in all the people whom I saw—there were many of them, going to and fro busily—that they were receptive and reflecting beings. They differed greatly in the degree in which they gave this impression; but all gave it. Some were quite pale, though pure in color; others glowed and shone. Yet when I say color, I use an earthly word, which does not express my meaning. It was more the atmosphere or penumbra, in which each moved, that I refer to, perhaps, than the tint of their bodies. They had bodies, very like such as I was used to. I saw that I myself was not, or so it appeared, greatly changed. I had form and dress, and I moved at will, and experienced sensations of pleasure and, above all, of magnificent health. For a while I was absorbed, without investigating details, in the mere sense of physical ease and power. I did not wish to speak, or to be spoken to, nor even to stir and exercise my splendid strength. It was more than enough to feel it, after all those weeks of pain. I lay back again upon the mignonette; as I did so, I noticed that the flowers where my form had pressed them were not bruised; they had sprung erect again; they had not wilted, nor even hung their heads as if they were hurt—I lay back upon, and deep within, the mignonette, and, drowned in the delicate odor, gazed about me.

Yes; I was truly in a wonderful place. It was in the country (as we should say below), though I saw signs of large centres of life, outlines of distant architecture far away. There were hills, and vast distances, and vistas of hill tints in the atmosphere. There were forests of great depth. There was an expanse of shining water. There were fields of fine extent and color, undulating like green seas. The sun was high—if it were the sun. At least there was great brilliance about me. Flowers must have been abundant, for the air was alive with perfumes.

When I have said this, I seem to have said little or nothing. Certain it is that these first impressions came to me in broad masses, like the sweep of a large brush or blender upon canvas. Of details I received few, for a long time. I was overcome with a sense of Nature—freedom—health—beauty, as if—how shall I say it?—as if for the first time I understood what generic terms meant; as if I had entered into the secret of all abstract glory; as if what we had known as philosophical or as poetical phrases were now become attainable facts, each possessing that individual existence in which dreamers upon earth dare to believe, and of which no doubter can be taught.

I am afraid I do not express this with anything like the simplicity with which I felt it; and to describe it with anything resembling the power would be impossible.

I felt my smallness and ignorance in view of the wonders which lay before me. "I shall have time enough to study them," I thought, but the thought itself thrilled me throughout, and proved far more of an excitant than a sedative. I rose slowly, and stood trembling among the mignonette. I shielded my eyes with my hand, not from any glare or dazzle or strain, but only from the presence and the pressure of beauty, and so stood looking off. As I did so, certain words came to mind with the haunting voice of a broken quotation:

"Neither have entered into the heart of man"—
"The things which God hath prepared"—

It was a relief to me to see my father coming towards me at that moment, for I had, perhaps, undergone as much keen emotion as one well bears, compressed into a short space of time. He met me smiling.

"And how is it, Mary?"

"My first Bible verse has just occurred to me, Father—the first religious thought I've had in Heaven yet!" I tried to speak lightly, feeling too deeply for endurance. I repeated the words to him, for he asked me what they were which had come to me.

"That is a pleasant experience," he said quietly. "It differs with us all. I have seen people enter in a transport of haste to see the Lord Himself—noticing nothing, forgetting everything. I have seen others come in a transport of terror—so afraid they were of Him."

"And I had scarcely thought about seeing Him till now!" I felt ashamed of this. But my father comforted me by a look.

"Each comes to his own by his own," he said. "The nature is never forced. Here we unfold like a leaf, a flower. He expects nothing of us but to be natural."

This seemed to me a deep saying; and the more I thought of it the deeper it seemed. I said so as we walked, separate still from the others, through the beautiful weather. The change from a New England winter to the climate in which I found myself was, in itself, not the least of the great effects and delights which I experienced that first day.

If nothing were expected of us but to be natural, it was the more necessary that it should be natural to be right.

I felt the full force of this conviction as it had never been possible to feel it in the other state of being, where I was under restraint. The meaning of *liberty* broke upon me like a sunburst. Freedom was in and of itself the highest law. Had I thought that death was to mean release from personal obedience? Lo, death itself was but the elevation of moral claims, from lower to higher. I perceived how all demands of the larger upon the lesser self must be increased in the condition to which I had arrived. I felt overpowered for the moment with the intensity of these claims. It seemed to me that I had never really known before, what obligation meant. Conduct was now the least of difficulties. For impulse, which lay behind conduct, for all force which wrought out fact in me, I had become accountable.

"As nearly as I can make it out, Father," I said, "henceforth I shall be responsible for my nature."

"Something like that; not altogether."

"The force of circumstance and heredity,"—I began, using the old earthly *patois*. "Of course I'm not to be called to account for what I start with here, any more than I was for what I started with there. That would be neither science nor philosophy."

"We are neither unscientific nor unphilosophical, you will find," said my father, patiently.

"I am very dull, sir. Be patient with me. What I am trying to say, I believe, is that I shall feel the deepest mortification if I do not find it natural to do right. This feeling is so keen, that to be wrong must be the most unnatural thing in the world. There is certainly a great difference from what it used to be; I cannot explain it. Already I am ashamed of the smallness of my thoughts when I first looked about in this place. Already I cannot understand why I did not spring like a fountain to the Highest, to the Best. But then, Father, I never was a devotee, you know."

When I had uttered these words I felt a recoil from myself, and sense of discord. I was making excuses for myself. That used to be a fault of the past life. One did not do it here. It was as if I had committed some grave social indecorum. I felt myself blushing. My father noticed my embarrassment, and called my attention to a brook by which we were walking, beginning to talk of its peculiar translucence and rhythm, and other little novelties, thus kindly diverting me from my distress, and teaching me how we were spared everything we could be in heaven, even in trifles like this. I was not so much as permitted to bear the edge of my regret, without the velvet of tenderness interposing to blunt the smart. It used to be thought among us below that one must be allowed to suffer from error, to learn. It seemed to be found here, that one learned by being saved from suffering. I wondered how it would be in the case of a really grave wrong which I might be so miserable as to commit; and if I should ever be so unfortunate as to discover by personal experience.

This train of thought went on while I was examining the brook. It had brilliant colors in the shallows, where certain strange agates formed pebbles of great beauty. There were also shells. A brook with shells enchanted me. I gathered some of them; they had opaline tints, and some were transparent as spun glass; they glittered in the hand, and did not dull when out of the water, like the shells we were used to. The shadows of strange trees hung across the tiny brown current, and unfamiliar birds flashed like tossed jewels overhead, through the branches and against the wonderful color of the sky. The birds were singing. One among them had a marvelous note. I listened to it for some time before I discovered that this bird was singing a Te Deum. How I knew that it was a Te Deum I cannot say. The others were more like earthly birds, except for the thrilling sweetness of their notes—and I could not see this one, for she seemed to be hidden from sight upon her nest. I observed that the bird upon the nest sang here as well as that upon the bough; and that I understood her: "*Te Deum laudamus—laudamus*" as distinctly as if I had been listening to a human voice.

When I had comprehended this, and stood entranced to listen, I began to catch the same melody in the murmur of the water, and perceived, to my astonishment, that the two, the brook and the bird, carried parts of the harmony of a solemn and majestic mass. Apparently these were but portions of the whole, but all which it was permitted me to hear. My father explained to me that it was not every natural beauty which had the power to join in such surpassing chorals; these were selected, for reasons which he did not attempt to specify. I surmised that they were some of the simplest of the wonders of this mythical world, which were entrusted to new-comers, as being first within the range of their capacities. I was enraptured with what I heard. The light throbbed about me. The sweet harmony rang on. I bathed my face in the musical water—it was as if I absorbed the sound at the pores of my skin. Dimly I received a hint of the possible existence of a sense or senses of which I had never heard.

What wonders were to come! What knowledge, what marvel, what stimulation and satisfaction! And I had but just begun! I was overwhelmed with this thought, and looked about; I knew not which way to turn; I had not what to say. Where was the first step? What was the next delight? The fire of discovery kindled in my veins. Let us hasten, that we may investigate Heaven!

"Shall we go on?" asked Father, regarding me earnestly.

"Yes, yes!" I cried, "let us go on. Let us see more—learn all. What a world have I come to! Let us begin at the beginning, and go to the end of it! Come quickly!"

I caught his hand, and we started on my eager mood. I felt almost a superabundance of vitality, and sprang along; there was everlasting health within my bounding arteries; there was eternal vigor in my firm muscle and sinews. How shall I express, to one who has never experienced it, the consciousness of life that can never die?

I could have leaped, flown, or danced like a child. I knew not how to walk sedately, like others whom I saw about us, who looked at me smiling, as older people look at the young on earth. "I, too, have felt thus—and thus." I wanted to exercise the power of my arms and limbs. I longed to test the triumphant poise of my nerve. My brain grew clearer and clearer, while for the gladness in my heart there is not any earthly word. As I bounded on, I looked more curiously at the construction of the body in which I found myself. It was, and yet it was not, like that which I had worn on earth. I seemed to have slipped out of one garment into another. Perhaps it was nearer the truth to say that it was like casting off an outer for an inner dress. There were nervous and arterial and other systems, it seemed, to which I had been accustomed. I cannot explain wherein they differed, as they surely did, and did enormously, from their representatives below. If I say that I felt as if I had got into the *soul of a body*, shall I be understood? It was as if I had been encased, one body within the other, to use a small earthly comparison, like the ivory figures which curious Chinese carvers cut within temple windows.

I was constantly surprised at this. I do not know what I had expected, but assuredly nothing like the fact. Vague visions of gaseous or meteoric angelic forms have their place in the imaginations of most of us below; we picture our future selves as a kind of nebulosity. When I felt the spiritual flesh, when I used the strange muscle, when I heard the new heart-beat of my heavenly identity, I remembered certain words, with a sting of mortification that I had known them all my life, and paid so cool a heed to them: "There is a terrestrial body, and there is a celestial body." The glory of the terrestrial was one. Behold, the glory of the celestial was another. St. Paul had set this tremendous assertion revolving in the sky of the human mind, like a star which we had not brought into our astronomy.

It was not a hint or a hope that he gave; it was the affirmation of a man who presumed to know. In common with most of his readers, I had received his statement with a poor incredulity or cold disregard. Nothing in the whole range of what we used to call the Bible, had been more explicit than those words; neither metaphor, nor allegory, nor parable befogged them; they were as clear cut as the dictum of Descartes. I recalled them with confusion, as I bounded over the elastic and wondrously-tinted grass.

Never before, at least, had I known what the color of green should be; resembling, while differing from that called by the name on earth—a development of a color, a blossom from a bud, a marvel from a commonplace. Thus the sweet and common clothing which God had given to our familiar earth, transfigured, wrapped again the hills and fields of Heaven. And oh, what else? what next? I turned to my father to ask him in which direction we were going; at this moment an arrest of the whole current of feeling checked me like a great dam.

Up to this point I had gone dizzily on; I had experienced the thousand diversions of a traveler in a foreign land; and, like such a traveler, I had become oblivious of that which I had left. The terrible incapacity of the human mind to retain more than one class of strong impressions at once, was temporarily increased by the strain of this, the greatest of all human experiences. The new had expelled the old. In an intense revulsion of feeling, too strong for expression, I turned my back on the beautiful landscape. All Heaven was before me, but dear, daily love was behind.

"Father," I said, choking, "I never forgot them before in all my life. Take me home! Let me go at once. I am not fit to be alive if Heaven itself can lead me to neglect my mother."

IV.

IN my distress I turned and would have fled, which way I knew not. I was swept up like a weed on a surge of self-reproach and longing. What was eternal life if she had found out that I was dead? What were the splendors of Paradise, if she missed me? It was made evident to me that my father was gratified at the turn my impulses had taken, but he intimated that it might not be possible to follow them, and that this was a matter which must be investigated before acting. This surprised me, and I inquired of him eagerly— yet, I think not passionately, not angrily, as I should once have done at the thwarting of such a wish as that—what he meant by the doubt he raised.

"It is not always permitted," he said gravely. "We cannot return when we would. We go upon these errands when it is Willed. I will go and learn what the Will may be for you touching this matter. Stay here and wait for me."

Before I could speak, he had departed swiftly, with the great and glad motion of those who go upon sure business in this happy place; as if he himself, at least, obeyed unseen directions, and obeyed them with his whole being. To me, so lately from a lower life, and still so choked with its errors, this loving obedience of the soul to a great central Force which I felt on every hand, but comprehended not, as yet, affected me like the discovery of a truth in science. It was as if I had found a new law of gravitation, to be mastered only by infinite attention. I fell to thinking more quietly after my father had left me alone. There came a subsidence to my tempestuous impulse, which astonished myself. I felt myself drawn and shaped, even like a wave by the tide, by something mightier far than my own wish. But there was this about the state of feeling into which I had come: that which controlled me was not only greater, it was dearer than my desire. Already a calmness conquered my storm. Already my heart awaited, without outburst or out-thrust, the expression of that other desire which should decide my fate in this most precious matter. All the old rebellion was gone, even as the protest of a woman goes on earth before the progress of a mighty love. I no longer argued and explained. I did not require or insist. Was it possible that I did not even doubt? The mysterious, celestial law of gravitation grappled me. I could no more presume to understand it than I could withstand it.

I had not been what is called a submissive person. All my life, obedience had torn me in twain. Below, it had cost me all I had to give, to cultivate what believers called trust in God.

I had indeed tried, in a desperate and faulty fashion, but I had often been bitterly ashamed at the best result which I could achieve, feeling that I scarcely deserved to count myself among His children, or to call myself by the Name which represented the absolute obedience of the strongest nature that human history had known. Always, under all, I had doubted whether I accepted God's will because I wanted to, so much as because I had to. This fear had given me much pain, but being of an active temperament, far, perhaps too far, removed from mysticism, I had gone on to the next fight, or the next duty, without settling my difficulties; and so like others of my sort, battled along through life, as best or as worst I might. I had always hurried more than I had grown. To be sure, I was not altogether to blame for this, since circumstances had driven me fast, and I had yielded to them not always for my own sake; but clearly, it may be as much of a misfortune to be too busy, as to be idle; and one whose subtlest effects are latest perceived. I could now understand it to be reasonable, that if I had taken more time on earth to cultivate myself for the conditions of Heaven, I might have had a different experience at the outset of this life, in which one was never in a hurry.

My father returned from his somewhat protracted absence, while I was thinking of these things thus quietly. My calmer mood went out to meet his face, from which I saw at once what was the result of his errand, and so a gentle process prepared me for my disappointment when he said that it was not Willed that I should go to her at this immediate time. He advised me to rest awhile before taking the journey, and to seek this rest at once. No reasons were given for this command; yet strangely, I felt it to be the most reasonable thing in the world.

No; blessedly no! I did not argue, or protest, I did not dash out my wild wish, I did not ask or answer anything—how wonderful!

Had I needed proof any longer that I was dead and in Heaven, this marvelous adjustment of my will to that other would in itself have told me what and where I was.

I cannot say that this process took place without effort. I found a certain magnificent effort in it, like that involved in the free use of my muscles; but it took place without pain. I did indeed ask,—

"Will it be long?"

"Not long."

"That is kind in Him!" I remember saying, as we moved away. For now, I found that I thought first rather of what He gave than of what He denied. It seemed to me that I had acquired a new instinct. My being was larger by the acquisition of a fresh power. I felt a little as I used to do below, when I had conquered a new language.

I had met, and by his loving mercy I had mastered, my first trial in the eternal life. This was to be remembered. It was like the shifting of a plate upon a camera.

More wearied than I had thought by the effort, I was glad to sink down beneath the trees in a nook my father showed me, and yield to the drowsiness that stole upon me after the great excitement of the day. It was not yet dark, but I was indeed tired. A singular subsidence, not like our twilight, but still reminding one of it, had fallen upon the vivid color of the air. No one was passing; the spot was secluded; my father bade me farewell for the present, saying that he should return again; and I was left alone.

The grass was softer than eider of the lower world; and lighter than snow-flakes, the leaves that fell from low-hanging boughs about me. Distantly, I heard moving water; and more near, sleepy birds. More distant yet, I caught, and lost, and caught again, fragments of orchestral music. I felt infinite security. I had the blessedness of weariness that knew it could not miss of sleep. Dreams stole upon me with motion and touch so exquisite that I thought: "Sleep itself is a new joy; what we had below was only a hint of the real thing," as I sank into deep and deeper rest.

Do not think that I forgot my love and longing to be elsewhere. I think the wish to see her and to comfort her grew clearer every moment. But stronger still, like a comrade marching beside it, I felt the pacing of that great desire which had become dearer than my own.

V.

WHEN I waked, I was still alone. There seemed to have been showers, for the leaves and grass about me were wet; yet I felt no chill or dampness, or any kind of injury from this fact. Rather I had a certain refreshment, as if my sleeping senses had drunk of the peace and power of the dew that flashed far and near about me. The intense excitement under which I had labored since coming to this place was calmed. All the fevers of feeling were laid. I could not have said whether there had been what below we called night, or how the passage of time had marked itself; I only knew that I had experienced the recuperation of night, and that I sprang to the next duty or delight of existence with the vigor of recurring day.

As I rose from the grass, I noticed a four-leaved clover, and remembering the pretty little superstition we used to have about it, I plucked it, and held it to my face, and so learned that the rain-drop in this new land had perfume; an exquisite scent; as if into the essence of brown earth and spicy roots, and aromatic green things, such as summer rain distills with us from out a fresh-washed world, there were mingled an inconceivable odor drawn out of the heart of the sky. Metaphysicians used to tell us that no man ever imagined a new perfume, even in his dreams. I could see that they were right, for anything like the perfume of clover after a rain in Heaven, had never entered into my sense or soul before. I saved the clover "for good luck," as I used to do.

Overhead there was a marvel. There seemed to have been clouds—their passing and breaking, and flitting—and now, behold the heavens themselves, bared of all their storm-drapery, had drawn across their dazzling forms a veil of glory. From what, for want of better knowledge, I still called East to West, and North to South, one supernal prism swept. The whole canopy of the sky was a rainbow.

It is impossible to describe this sight in any earthly tongue, to any dwellers of the earth. I stood beneath it, as a drop stands beneath the ocean. For a time I could only feel the surge of beauty—mere beauty—roll above me. Then, I think, as the dew had fallen from the leaf, so I sunk upon my knees. I prayed because it was natural to pray, and felt God in my soul as the prism feels the primary color, while I thanked Him that I was immortally alive. It had never been like this before, to pray; nay, prayer itself was now one of the discoveries of Heaven. It throbbed through me like the beat of a new heart. It seemed to me that He must be very near me. Almost it was, as if He and I were alone together in the Universe. For the first time, the passionate wish to be taken into His very visible presence,—that intense desire which I had heard of, as overpowering so many of the newly dead,—

began to take possession of me. But I put it aside, since it was not permitted, and a consciousness of my unfitness came to me, that made the wish itself seem a kind of mistake. I think this feeling was not unlike what we called below a sense of sin. I did not give it that name at that time. It had come to me so naturally and gradually, that there was no strain or pain about it. Yet when I had it, I could no longer conceive of being without it. It seemed to me that I was a stronger and wiser woman for it. A certain gentleness and humility different from what I had been used to, in my life of activity, wherein so many depended on me, and on the decided faculties of my nature, accompanied the growing sense of personal unworthiness with which I entered on the blessedness of everlasting life.

I watched the rainbow of the sky till it had begun to fade—an event in itself an exquisite wonder, for each tint of the prism flashed out and ran in lightning across the heavens before falling to its place in the primary color, till at last the whole spectacle was resolved into the three elements, the red, the yellow, and the blue; which themselves moved on and away, like a conqueror dismissing a pageant.

When this gorgeous scene had ended, I was surprised to find that though dead and in Heaven, I was hungry. I gathered fruits which grew near, of strange form and flavor, but delicious to the taste past anything I had ever eaten, and I drank of the brook where the shells were, feeling greatly invigorated thereby. I was beginning to wonder where my father was, when I saw him coming towards me. He greeted me with his old good-morning kiss, laying his hand upon my head in a benediction that filled my soul.

As we moved on together, I asked him if he remembered how we used to say below:

"What a heavenly day!"

Many people seemed to be passing on the road which we had chosen, but as we walked on they grew fewer.

"There are those who wish to speak with you," he said with a slight hesitation, "but all things can wait here; we learn to wait ourselves. You are to go to your mother now."

"And not with you?" I asked, having a certain fear of the mystery of my undertaking. He shook his head with a look more nearly like disappointment than anything I had seen upon his face in this new life; explaining to me, however, with cheerful acquiescence, that it was not Willed that he should join me on my journey.

"Tell her that I come shortly," he added, "and that I come alone. She will understand. And have no fear; you have much to learn, but it will come syllable by syllable."

Now swiftly, at the instant while he spoke with me, I found myself alone and in a mountainous region, from which a great outlook was before me. I saw the kingdoms of heaven and the glory of them, spread out before me like a map. A mist of the colors of amethyst and emerald interfused, enwrapped the outlines of the landscape. All details grew blurred and beautiful like a dream at which one snatches vainly in the morning. Off, and beyond, the infinite ether throbbed. Yonder, like a speck upon a sunbeam, swam the tiny globe which we called earth. Stars and suns flashed and faded, revolving and waiting in their places. Surely it was growing dark, for they sprang out like mighty light-houses upon the grayness of the void.

The splendors of the Southern cross streamed far into the strange light, neither of night nor day, not of twilight or dawn, which surrounded me.

Colored suns, of which astronomers had indeed taught us, poured undreamed-of light upon unknown planets. I passed worlds whose luminaries gave them scarlet, green, and purple days. "These too," I thought, "I shall one day visit." I flashed through currents of awful color, and measures of awful night. I felt more than I perceived, and wondered more than I feared. It was some moments before I realized, by these few astronomical details, that I was adrift, alone upon the mystery and mightiness of Space.

Of this strange and solitary journey, I can speak so imperfectly, that it were better almost to leave it out of my narrative. Yet, when I remember how I have sometimes heard those still upon earth conceive, with the great fear and ignorance inseparable from earth-trained imagination, of such transits of the soul from point to point in ether, I should be glad to express at least the incomplete impressions which I received from this experience.

The strongest of these, and the sweetest, was the sense of safety—and still the sense of safety; unassailable, everlasting; blessed beyond the thought of an insecure life to compass. To be dead was to be dead to danger, dead to fear. To be dead was to be alive to a sense of assured good chance that nothing in the universe could shake.

So I felt no dread, believe me, though much awe and amazement, as I took my first journey from Heaven to earth. I have elsewhere said that the distance, by astronomical calculation, was in itself perhaps not enormous. I had an impression that I was crossing a great sphere or penumbra, belonging to the earth itself, and having a certain relation to it, like the soul to the body of a man.

Was Heaven located within or upon this world-soul? The question occurred to me, but up to this time, I am still unable to answer it. The transit itself was swift and subtle as a thought. Indeed, it seemed to me that thought itself might have been my vehicle of conveyance; or perhaps I should say, feeling. My love and longing took me up like pollen taken by the wind. As I approached the spot where my dear ones dwelt and sorrowed for me, desire and speed both increased by a mighty momentum.

Now I did not find this journey as difficult as that other, when I had departed, a freshly-freed soul, from earth to Heaven. I learned that I was now subject to other natural laws. A celestial gravitation controlled the celestial body, as that of the earth had compelled the other. I was upborne in space by this new and mysterious influence. Yet there was no dispute between it and the other law, the eternal law of love, which drew me down. Between soul and body, in the heavenly existence, there could be no more conflict than between light and an ether wave.

I do not say that I performed this journey without effort or intelligence. The little knowledge I ever had was taxed in view of the grandeurs and the mysteries around me. Shall I be believed if I say that I recalled all the astronomy and geography that my life as a teacher had left still somewhat freshly imprinted on the memory? that the facts of physics recurred to me, even in that inroad of feeling? and that I guided myself to the Massachusetts town as I would have found it upon a globe at school? Already I learned that no acquisition of one life is lost in the next. Already I thanked God for everything I knew, only wishing, with the passion of ignorance newly revealed to itself by the dawn of wisdom, that my poor human acquirements had ever truly deserved the high name of study, or stored my thought with its eternal results.

VI.

AS I approached the scene of my former life, I met many people. I had struck a realm of spirits who at first perplexed me. They did not look happy, and seemed possessed by great unrest. I observed that, though they fluttered and moved impatiently, none rose far above the surface of the earth. Most of them were employed in one way or another upon it. Some bought and sold; some eat and drank; others occupied themselves in coarse pleasures, from which one could but turn away the eyes. There were those who were busied in more refined ways:—students with eyes fastened to dusty volumes; virtuosos who hung about a picture, a statue, a tapestry, that had enslaved them; one musical creature I saw, who ought to have been of exquisite organization, judging from his hands—he played perpetually upon an instrument that he could not tune; women, I saw too, who robed and disrobed without a glint of pleasure in their faded faces.

There were ruder souls than any of these—but one sought for them in the dens of the earth; their dead hands still were red with stains of blood, and in their dead hearts reigned the remnants of hideous passions.

Of all these appearances, which I still found it natural to call phenomena as I should once have done, it will be remembered that I received the temporary and imperfect impression of a person passing swiftly through a crowd, so that I do not wish my account to be accepted for anything more trustworthy than it is.

While I was wondering greatly what it meant, some one joined and spoke to me familiarly, and, turning, I saw it to be that old neighbor, Mrs. Mersey, to whom I have alluded, who, like myself, seemed to be bent upon an errand, and to be but a visitor upon the earth. She was a most lovely spirit, as she had always been, and I grasped her hand cordially while we swept on rapidly together to our journey's end.

"Do tell me," I whispered, as soon as I could draw her near enough, "who all these people are, and what it means. I fear to guess. And yet indeed they seem like the dead who cannot get away."

"Alas," she sighed, "you have said it. They loved nothing, they lived for nothing, they believed in nothing, they cultivated themselves for nothing but the earth. They simply lack the spiritual momentum to get away from it. It is as much the working of a natural law as the progress of a fever. Many of my duties have been among such as these. I know them well. They need time and tact in treatment, and oh, the greatest patience! At first it discouraged me, but I am learning the enthusiasm of my work."

"These, then," I said, "were those I saw in that first hour, when my father led me out of the house, and through the street. I saw you among them, Mrs. Mersey, but I knew even then that you were not of them. But surely they do not stay forever prisoners of the earth? Surely such a blot on the face of spiritual life cannot but fade away? I am a new-comer. I am still quite ignorant, you see. But I do not understand, any more than I did before, how that could be."

"They have their choice," she answered vaguely. But when I saw the high solemnity of her aspect, I feared to press my questions. I could not, however, or I did not forbear saying:—

"At least *you* must have already persuaded many to sever themselves from such a condition as this?"

"Already some, I hope," she replied evasively, as she moved away. She always had remarkably fine manners, of which death had by no means deprived her. I admired her graciousness and dignity as she passed from my side to that of one we met, who, in a dejected voice, called her by her name, and intimated that he wished to speak with her. He was a pale and restless youth, and I thought, but was not sure, for we separated so quickly, that it was the little fellow I spoke of, Bobby Bend. I looked back, after I had advanced some distance on my way, and saw the two together, conversing earnestly. While I was still watching them, it seemed to me, though I cannot be positive upon this point, that they had changed their course, and were quietly ascending, she leading, he following, above the dismal sphere in which she found the lad, and that his heavy, awkward, downward motions became freer, struggling upward, as I gazed.

I had now come to the location of my old home, and, as I passed through the familiar village streets, I saw that night was coming on. I met many whom I knew, both of those called dead and living. The former recognized me, but the latter saw me not. No one detained me, however, for I felt in haste which I could not conceal.

With high-beating heart, I approached the dear old house. No one was astir. As I turned the handle of the door, a soft, sickening touch crawled around my wrist; recoiling, I found that I was entwisted in a piece of crape that the wind had blown against me.

I went in softly; but I might have spared myself the pains. No one heard me, though the heavy door creaked, I thought, as emphatically as it always had—loudest when we were out latest, and longest when we shut it quickest. I went into the parlor and stood, for a moment, uncertain what to do.

Alice was there, and my married sister Jane, with her husband and little boy. They sat about the fire, conversing sadly. Alice's pretty eyes were disfigured with crying. They spoke constantly of me. Alice was relating to Jane and her family the particulars of my illness. I was touched to hear her call me "patient and sweet;"—none the less because she had often told me I was the most impatient member of the family.

No one had observed my entrance. Of course I was prepared for this, but I cannot tell why I should have felt it, as I certainly did. A low bamboo chair, cushioned with green *crétonne*, stood by the table. I had a fancy for this chair, and, pleased that they had left it unoccupied, advanced and took it, in the old way. It was with something almost like a shock, that I found myself unnoticed in the very centre of their group.

While I sat there, Jane moved to fix the fire, and, in returning, made as if she would take the bamboo chair.

"Oh, don't!" said Alice, sobbing freshly. Jane's own tears sprang, and she turned away.

"It seems to me," said my brother-in-law, looking about with the patient grimace of a business man compelled to waste time at a funeral, "that there has a cold draught come into this room from somewhere. Nobody has left the front door open, I hope? I'll go and see."

He went, glad of the excuse to stir about, poor fellow, and I presume he took a comfortable smoke outside.

The little boy started after his father, but was bidden back, and crawled up into the chair where I was sitting. I took the child upon my lap, and let him stay. No one removed him, he grew so quiet, and he was soon asleep in my arm. This pleased me; but I could not be contented long, so I kissed the boy and put him down. He cried bitterly, and ran to his mother for comfort.

While they were occupied with him, I stole away. I thought I knew where Mother would be, and was ashamed of myself at the reluctance I certainly had to enter my own room, under these exciting circumstances.

Conquering this timidity, as unwomanly and unworthy, I went up and opened the familiar door. I had begun to learn that neither sound nor sight followed my motions now, so that I was not surprised at attracting no attention from the lonely occupant of the room. I closed the door—from long habit I still made an effort to turn the latch softly—and resolutely examined what I saw.

My mother was there, as I had expected. The room was cold—there was no fire,—and she had on her heavy blanket shawl. The gas was lighted, and one of my red candles, but both burned dimly. The poor woman's magenta geranium had frozen. My mother sat in the red easy-chair, which, being a huge, old-fashioned thing, surrounded and shielded her from the draught. My clothes, and medicines, and all the little signs of sickness had been removed. The room was swept, and orderly. Above the bed, the pictures and the carved cross looked down.

Below them, calm as sleep, and cold as frost, and terrible as silence, lay that which had been I.

She did not shrink. She was sitting close beside it. She gazed at it with the tenderness which death itself could not affright. Mother was not crying. She did not look as if she had shed tears for a long time. But her wanness and the drawn lines about her mouth were hard to see. Her aged hands trembled as she cut the locks of hair from the neck of the dead. She was growing to be an old woman. And I—her first-born—I had been her staff of life, and on me she had thought to lean in her widowed age. She seemed to me to have grown feeble fast in the time since I had left her.

All my soul rushed to my lips, and I cried out—it seemed that either the dead or the living must hear that cry—

"Mother! Oh, my dear *mother*!"

But deaf as life, she sat before me. She had just cut off the lock of hair she wanted; as I spoke, the curling ends of it twined around her fingers; I tried to snatch it away, thinking thus to arrest her attention.

The lock of hair trembled, turned, and clung the closer to the living hand. She pressed it to her lips with the passion of desolation.

"But, Mother," I cried once more, "I am *here*." I flung my arms about her and kissed her again and again. I called and entreated her by every dear name that household love had taught us. I besought her to turn, to see, to hear, to believe, to be comforted. I told her how blest was I, how bountiful was death.

"I am alive," I said. "I am alive! I see you, I touch you, hear you, love you, hold you!" I tried argument and severity; I tried tenderness and ridicule.

She turned at this: it seemed to me that she regarded me. She stretched her arms out; her aged hands groped to and fro as if she felt for something and found it not; she shook her head, her dim eyes gazed blankly into mine. She sighed patiently, and rose as if to leave the room, but hesitated,—covered the face of the dead body—caressed it once or twice as if it had been a living infant—and then, taking up her Bible, which had been upon the chair beside her, dropped upon her knees, and holding the book against her sunken cheek, abandoned herself to silent prayer.

This was more than I could bear just then, and, thinking to collect myself by a few moments' solitude, I left her. But as I stood in the dark hall, uncertain and unquiet, I noticed a long, narrow line of light at my feet, and, following it confusedly, found that it came from the crack in the closed, but unlatched door of another well-remembered room. I pushed the door open hurriedly and closed it behind me.

My brother sat in this room alone. His fire was blazing cheerfully and, flashing, revealed the deer's-head from the Adirondacks, the stuffed rose-curlew from Florida, the gull's wing from Cape Ann, the gun and rifle and bamboo fish-pole, the class photographs over the mantel, the feminine features on porcelain in velvet frames, all the little trappings with which I was familiar. Tom had been trying to study, but his Homer lay pushed away, with crumpled leaves, upon the table. Buried in his lexicon—one strong elbow intervening—down, like a hero thrown, the boy's face had gone.

"Tom," I said quietly—I always spoke quietly to Tom, who had a constitutional fear of what he called "emotions"—"Tom, you'd better be studying your Greek. I'd much rather see you. Come, I'll help you."

He did not move, poor fellow, and as I came nearer, I saw, to my heart-break, that our Tom was crying. Sobs shook his huge frame, and down between the iron fingers, toughened by base-ball matches, tears had streamed upon the pages of the Odyssey.

"Tom, Tom, old fellow, *don't!*" I cried, and, hungry as love, I took the boy. I got upon the arm of the smoking chair, as I used to, and so had my hands about his neck, and my cheek upon his curly hair, and would have soothed him. Indeed, he did grow calm, and calmer, as if he yielded to my touch; and presently he lifted his wet face, and looked about the room, half ashamed, half defiant, as if to ask who saw that.

"Come, Tom," I tried again. "It really isn't so bad as you think. And there is Mother catching cold in that room. Go and get her away from the body. It is no place for her. She'll get sick. Nobody can manage her as well as you."

As if he heard me, he arose. As if he knew me, he looked for the flashing of an instant into my eyes.

"I don't see how a girl of her sense can be *dead*," said the boy aloud. He stretched his arms once above his head, and out into the bright, empty room, and I heard him groan in a way that wrung my heart. I went impulsively to him, and as his arms closed, they closed about me strongly. He stood for a moment quite still. I could feel the nervous strain subsiding all over his big soul and body.

"Hush," I whispered. "I'm no more dead than you are."

If he heard, what he felt, God knows. I speak of a mystery. No optical illusion, no tactual hallucination could hold the boy who took all the medals at the gymnasium. The hearty, healthy fellow could receive no abnormal sign from the love and longing of the dead. Only spirit unto spirit could attempt that strange out-reaching. Spirit unto spirit, was it done? Still, I relate a mystery, and what shall I say? His professor in the class-room of metaphysics would teach him next week that grief owns the law of the rhythm of motion; and that at the oscillation of the pendulum the excitement of anguish shall subside into apathy which mourners alike treat as a disloyalty to the dead, and court as a nervous relief to the living.

Be this as it may, the boy grew suddenly calm, and even cheerful, and followed me at once. I led him directly to his mother, and left them for a time alone together.

After this my own calm, because my own confidence, increased. My dreary sense of helplessness before the suffering of those I loved, gave place to the consciousness of power to reach them. I detected this power in myself in an undeveloped form, and realized that it might require exercise and culture, like all other powers, if I would make valuable use of it. I could already regard the cultivation of the faculty which would enable love to defy death, and spirit to conquer matter, as likely to be one of the occupations of a full life.

I went out into the fresh air for a time to think these thoughts through by myself, undisturbed by the sight of grief that I could not remove; and strolled up and down the village streets in the frosty night.

When I returned to the house they had all separated for the night, sadly seeking sleep in view of the events of the morrow, when, as I had already inferred, the funeral would take place.

I spent the night among them, chiefly with my mother and Tom, passing unnoticed from room to room, and comforting them in such ways as I found possible. The boy had locked his door, but after a few trials I found myself able to pass the medium of this resisting matter, and to enter and depart according to my will. Tom finished his lesson in the Odyssey, and I sat by and helped him when I could. This I found possible in simple ways, which I may explain farther at another time. We had often studied together, and his mind the more readily, therefore, responded to the influence of my own. He was soon well asleep, and I was free to give all my attention to my poor mother. Of those long and solemn hours, what shall I say? I thought she would never, never rest. I held her in these arms the live-long night. With these hands I caressed and calmed her. With these lips I kissed her. With this breath I warmed her cold brow and fingers. With all my soul and body I willed that I would comfort her, and I believe, thank God, I did. At dawn she slept peacefully; she slept late, and rose refreshed. I remained closely by her throughout the day.

They did their best, let me say, to provide me with a Christian funeral, partly in accordance with some wishes I had expressed in writing, partly from the impulse of their own good sense. Not a curtain was drawn to darken the house of death. The blessed winter sunshine flowed in like the current of a broad stream, through low, wide windows. No ghastly "funeral flowers" filled the room; there was only a cluster of red pinks upon the coffin, and the air was sweet but not heavy with the carnation perfume that they knew I loved. My dead body and face they had covered with a deep red pall, just shaded off the black, as dark as darkness could be, and yet be redness. Not a bell was tolled. Not a tear—at least, I mean, by those nearest me—not a tear was shed. As the body was carried from the house, the voices of unseen singers lifted the German funeral chant:—

"Go forth! go on, with solemn song,
Short is the way; the rest is long!"

At the grave they sang:—

"Softly now the light of day,"

since my mother had asked for one of the old hymns; and besides the usual Scriptural Burial Service, a friend, who was dear to me, read Mrs. Browning's "Sleep."

It was all as I would have had it, and I looked on peacefully. If I could have spoken I would have said: "You have buried me cheerfully, as Christians ought, as a Christian ought to be."

I was greatly touched, I must admit, at the grief of some of the poor, plain people who followed my body on its final journey to the village churchyard. The woman who sent the magenta geranium refused to be comforted, and there were one or two young girls whom I had been so fortunate as to assist in difficulties, who, I think, did truly mourn. Some of my boys from the Grand Army were there, too,—some, I mean, whom it had been my privilege to care for in the hospitals in the old war days. They came in uniform, and held their caps before their eyes. It did please me to see them there.

When the brief service at the grave was over, I would have gone home with my mother, feeling that she needed me more than ever; but as I turned to do so, I was approached by a spirit whose presence I had not observed. It proved to be my father. He detained me, explaining that I should remain where I was, feeling no fear, but making no protest, till the Will governing my next movement might be made known to me. So I bade my mother good-by, and Tom, as well as I could in the surprise and confusion, and watched them all as they went away. She, as she walked, seemed to those about her to be leaning only upon her son. But I beheld my father tenderly hastening close beside her, while he supported her with the arm which had never failed her yet, in all their loving lives. Therefore I could let her go, without distress.

The funeral procession departed slowly; the grave was filled; one of the mill-girls came back and threw in some arbor vitæ and a flower or two,—the sexton hurried her, and both went away. It grew dusk, dark. I and my body were left alone together.

Of that solemn watch, it is not for me to chatter to any other soul. Memories overswept me, which only we two could share. Hopes possessed me which it were not possible to explain to another organization. Regret, resolve, awe, and joy, every high human emotion excepting fear, battled about us. While I knelt there in the windless night, I heard chanting from a long distance, but yet distinct to the dead, that is to the living ear. As I listened, the sound deepened, approaching, and a group of singing spirits swept by in the starlit air, poised like birds, or thoughts, above me:

"It is sown a natural—it is raised a spiritual body."

"Death! where is thy sting?—Grave!—thy victory?"

"Believing in Me, though he were dead, yet shall he live."

I tried my voice, and joined, for I could no longer help it, in the thrilling chorus. It was the first time since I died, that I had felt myself invited or inclined to share the occupations of others, in the life I had entered. Kneeling there, in the happy night, by my own grave, I lifted all my soul and sense into the immortal words, now for the first time comprehensible to me:

"I believe, I believe in the resurrection of the dead."

It was not long thereafter that I received the summons to return. I should have been glad to go home once more, but was able to check my own preference without wilful protest, or an aching heart. The conviction that all was well with my darlings and myself, for life and for death, had now become an intense yet simple thing, like consciousness itself.

I went as, and where I was bidden, joyfully.

VII.

Upon reëntering the wonderful place which I had begun to call Heaven, and to which I still give that name, though not, I must say, with perfect assurance that the word is properly applied to that phase of the life of which I am the yet most ignorant recorder, I found myself more weary than I had been at any time since my change came. I was looking about, uncertain where to go, feeling, for the first time, rather homeless in this new country, when I was approached by a stranger, who inquired of me what I sought:

"Rest," I said promptly.

"A familiar quest," observed the stranger, smiling.

"You are right, sir. It is a thing I have been seeking for forty years."

"And never found?"

"Never found."

"I will assist you," he said gently, "that is, if you wish it. What will you have first?"

"Sleep, I think, first, then food. I have been through exciting scenes. I have a touch—a faint one—of what below we called exhaustion. Yet now I am conscious in advance of the rest which is sure to come. Already I feel it, like the ebbing of the wave that goes to form the flow of the next. How blessed to know that one *can't* be ill!"

"How do you know that?" asked my companion.

"On the whole, I don't know that I do," I answered, with embarrassment, "I suppose it is a remnant of one's old religious teaching: 'The inhabitant shall not say I am sick.' Surely there were such words."

"And you trusted them?" asked the stranger.

"The Bible was a hard book to accept," I said quickly, "I would not have you overestimate my faith. I tried to believe that it was God's message. I think I *did* believe it. But the reason was clear to me. I could not get past that if I wished to."

"What, then, was the reason," inquired my friend, solemnly, "why you trusted the message called the Word of God, as received by the believing among His children on earth?"

"Surely," I urged, "there is but one reason. I refer to the history of our Lord. I do not know whether all in this place are Christians; but I was one.—

Sir! I anticipate your question. I was a most imperfect, useless one—to my sorrow and my shame I say it—but, so far as I went, I was an honest one."

"Did you love Him?—Him whom you called Lord?" asked the stranger, with an air of reserve. I replied that I thought I could truly say that He was dear to me.

I began to be deeply moved by this conversation. I stole a look at the stranger, whom I had at first scarcely noticed, except as one among many passing souls. He was a man of surpassing majesty of mien, and for loveliness of feature I had seen no mortal to vie with him. "This," I thought, "must be one of the beings we called angels." Astonishing brightness rayed from him at every motion, and his noble face was like the sun itself. He moved beside me like any other spirit, and condescended to me so familiarly, yet with so unapproachable a dignity, that my heart went out to him as breath upon the air. It did not occur to me to ask him who he was, or whither he led me. It was enough that he led, and I followed without question or reply. We walked and talked for a long time together.

He renewed the conversation by asking me whether I had really staked my immortal existence upon the promise of that obscure, uneducated Jew, twenty centuries in his grave,—that plain man who lived a fanatic's life, and died a felon's death, and whose teachings had given rise to such bigotry and error upon the earth. I answered that I had never been what is commonly called a devout person, not having a spiritual temperament, but that I had not held our Master responsible for the mistakes of either his friends or his foes, and that the greatest regret I had brought with me into Heaven was that I had been so unworthy to bear His blessed name. He next inquired of me, if I truly believed that I owed my entrance upon my present life to the interposition of Him of whom we spoke.

"Sir," I said, "you touch upon sacred nerves. I should find it hard to tell you how utterly I believe that immortality is the gift of Jesus Christ to the human soul."

"I believed this on earth," I added, "I believe it in Heaven. I do not *know* it yet, however. I am a new-comer; I am still very ignorant. No one has instructed me. I hope to learn 'syllable by syllable.' I am impatient to be taught; yet I am patient to be ignorant till I am found worthy to learn. It may be, that you, sir, who evidently are of a higher order of life than ours, are sent to enlighten me?"

My companion smiled, neither dissenting from, nor assenting to my question, and only asked me in reply, if I had yet spoken with the Lord. I said that I had not even seen Him; nay, that I had not even asked to see Him. My friend inquired why this was, and I told him frankly that it was partly because I was so occupied at first—nay, most of the time until I was called below.

"I had not much room to think. I was taken from event to event, like a traveler. This matter that you speak of seemed out of place in every way at that time."

Then I went on to say that my remissness was owing partly to a little real self-distrust, because I feared I was not the kind of believer to whom He would feel quickly drawn; that I felt afraid to propose such a preposterous thing as being brought into His presence; that I supposed, when He saw fit to reveal Himself to me, I should be summoned in some orderly way, suitable to this celestial community; that, in fact, though I had cherished this most sweet and solemn desire, I had not mentioned it before, not even to my own father who conducted me to this place.

"I have not spoken of it," I said, "to any body but to you."

The stranger's face wore a remarkable expression when I said this, as if I had deeply gratified him; and there glittered from his entire form and features such brightness as well-nigh dazzled me. It was as if, where a lesser being would have spoken, or stirred, he shone. I felt as if I conversed with him by radiance, and that living light had become a vocabulary between us. I have elsewhere spoken of the quality of reflecting light as marked among the ordinary inhabitants of this new life; but in this case I was aware of a distinction, due, I thought, to the superior order of existence to which my friend belonged. He did not, like the others, reflect; he radiated glory. More and more, as we had converse together, this impressed, until it awed me. We remained together for a long time. People who met us, greeted the angel with marked reverence, and turned upon me glances of sympathetic delight; but no one interrupted us. We continued our walk into a more retired place, by the shore of a sea, and there we had deep communion.

My friend had inquired if I were still faint, and if I preferred to turn aside for food and rest; but when he asked me the question I was amazed to find that I no longer had the need of either. Such delight had I in his presence, such invigoration in his sympathy, that glorious recuperation had set in upon my earth-caused weariness. Such power had the soul upon the celestial body! Food for the first was force to the other.

It seemed to me that I had never known refreshment of either before; and that Heaven itself could contain no nutriment that would satisfy me after this upon which I fed in that high hour.

It is not possible for me to repeat the solemn words of that interview. We spoke of grave and sacred themes. He gave me great counsel and fine sympathy. He gave me affectionate rebuke and unfathomable resolve. We talked of those inner experiences which, on earth, the soul protects, like struggling flame, between itself and the sheltering hand of God. We spoke much of the Master, and of my poor hope that I might be permitted after I had been a long time in Heaven, to become worthy to see Him, though at the vast distance of my unworthiness. Of that unworthiness too, we spoke most earnestly; while we did so, the sense of it grew within me like a new soul; yet so divinely did my friend extend his tenderness to me, that I was strengthened far more than weakened by these finer perceptions of my unfitness, which he himself had aroused in me. The counsel that he gave me, Eternity could not divert out of my memory, and the comfort which I had from him I treasure to this hour. "Here," I thought, "here, at last, I find reproof as gentle as sympathy, and sympathy as invigorating as reproof. Now, for the first time in all my life, I find myself truly understood. What could I not become if I possessed the friendship of such a being! How shall I develop myself so as to obtain it? How can I endure to be deprived of it? Is this too, like friendship on earth, a snatch, a compromise, a heart-ache, a mirror in which one looks only long enough to know that it is dashed away? Have I begun that old pain again, *here*?"

For I knew, as I sat in that solemn hour with my face to the sea and my soul with him, while sweeter than any song of all the waves of Heaven or earth to sea-lovers sounded his voice who did commune with me,—verily I knew, for then and forever, that earth had been a void to me because I had him not, and that Heaven could be no Heaven to me without him.

All which I had known of human love; all that I had missed; the dreams from which I had been startled; the hopes that had evaded me; the patience which comes from knowing that one may not even try not to be misunderstood; the struggle to keep a solitary heart sweet; the anticipation of desolate age which casts its shadow backward upon the dial of middle life; the paralysis of feeling which creeps on with its disuse; the distrust of one's own atrophied faculties of loving; the sluggish wonder if one is ceasing to be lovable; the growing difficulty of explaining oneself even when it is necessary, because no one being more than any other cares for the explanation; the things which a lonely life converts into silence that cannot be broken, swept upon me like rapids, as, turning to look into his dazzling face, I said: "This—*all* this he understands."

But when, thus turning, I would have told him so, for there seemed to be no poor pride in Heaven, forbidding soul to tell the truth to soul,—when I turned, my friend had risen, and was departing from me, as swiftly and mysteriously as he came. I did not cry out to him to stay, for I felt ashamed; nor did I tell him how he had bereft me, for that seemed a childish folly. I think I only stood and looked at him.

"If there is any way of being worthy of your friendship," I said below my breath, "I will have it, if I toil for half Eternity to get it."

Now, though these words were scarcely articulate, I think he heard them, and turning, with a smile which will haunt my dreams and stir my deeds as long as I shall live, he laid his hand upon my head, and blessed me—but what he said I shall tell no man—and so departed from me, and I was left upon the shore alone, fallen, I think, in a kind of sleep or swoon.

When I awoke, I was greatly calmed and strengthened, but disinclined, at first, to move. I had the reaction from what I knew was the intensest experience of my life, and it took time to adjust my feelings to my thoughts.

A young girl came up while I sat there upon the sands, and employed herself in gathering certain marvelous weeds that the sea had tossed up. These weeds fed upon the air, as they had upon the water, remaining fresh upon the girl's garments, which she decorated with them. She did not address me, but strolled up and down silently. Presently, feeling moved by the assurance of congeniality that one detects so much more quickly in Heaven than on earth, I said to the young girl:—

"Can you tell me the name of the angel—you must have met him—who has but just left me, and with whom I have been conversing?"

"Do you then truly not know?" she asked, shading her eyes with her hand, and looking off in the direction my friend had taken; then back again, with a fine, compassionate surprise at me.

"Indeed I know not."

"That was the Master who spoke with you."

"What did you *say*?"

"That was our Lord Himself."

VIII.

AFTER the experience related in the last chapter, I remained for some time in solitude. Speech seemed incoherence, and effort impossible. I needed a pause to adapt myself to my awe and my happiness; upon neither of which will it be necessary for me to dwell. Yet I think I may be understood if I say that from this hour I found that what we call Heaven had truly begun for me. Now indeed for the first time I may say that I believed without wonder in the life everlasting; since now, for the first time, I had a reason sufficient for the continuance of existence. A force like the cohesion of atoms held me to eternal hope. Brighter than the dawn of friendship upon a heart bereft, more solemn than the sunrise of love itself upon a life that had thought itself unloved, stole on the power of the Presence to which I had been admitted in so surprising, and yet, after all, how natural a way! Henceforth the knowledge that this experience might be renewed for me at any turn of thought or act, would illuminate joy itself, so that "it should have no need of the sun to lighten it." I recalled these words, as one recalls a familiar quotation repeated for the first time on some foreign locality of which it is descriptive. Now I knew what he meant, who wrote: "The Lamb is the Light thereof."

When I came to myself, I observed the young girl who had before addressed me still strolling on the shore. She beckoned, and I went to her, with a new meekness in my heart. What will He have me to do? If, by the lips of this young thing, He choose to instruct me, let me glory in the humility with which I will be a learner!

All things seemed to be so exquisitely ordered for us in this new life, all flowed so naturally, like one sound-wave into another, with ease so apparent, yet under law so superb, that already I was certain Heaven contained no accidents, and no trivialities; as it did no shocks or revolutions.

"If you like," said the young girl, "we will cross the sea."

"But how?" I asked, for I saw no boat.

"Can you not, then, walk upon the water yet?" she answered. "Many of us do, as He did once below. But we no longer call such things miracles. They are natural powers. Yet it is an art to use them. One has to learn it, as we did swimming, or such things, in the old times."

"I have only been here a short time," I said, half amused at the little celestial "airs" my young friend wore so sweetly. "I know but little yet. Can you teach me how to walk on water?"

"It would take so much time," said the young girl, "that I think we should not wait for that. We go on to the next duty, now. You had better learn, I think, from somebody wiser than I. I will take you over another way."

A great and beautiful shell, not unlike a nautilus, was floating near us, on the incoming tide, and my companion motioned to me to step into this. I obeyed her, laughing, but without any hesitation. "Neither shall there be any more death," I thought as I glanced over the rose-tinted edges of the frail thing into the water, deeper than any I had ever seen, but unclouded, so that I looked to the bottom of the sea. The girl herself stepped out upon the waves with a practiced air, and lightly drawing the great shell with one hand, bore me after her, as one bears a sledge upon ice. As we came into mid-water we began to meet others, some walking, as she did, some rowing or drifting like myself. Upon the opposite shore uprose the outlines of a more thickly settled community than any I had yet seen.

Watching this with interest that deepened as we approached the shore, I selfishly or uncourteously forgot to converse with my companion, who did not disturb my silence until we landed. As she gave me her hand, she said in a quick, direct tone:

"Well, Miss Mary, I see that you do not know me, after all."

I felt, as I had already done once or twice before, a certain social embarrassment (which in itself instructed me, as perpetuating one of the minor emotions of life below that I had hardly expected to renew) before my lovely guide, as I shook my head, struggling with the phantasmal memories evoked by her words. No, I did not know her.

"I am Marie Sauvée. I *hope* you remember."

She said these words in French. The change of language served instantly to recall the long train of impressions stored away, who knew how or where, about the name and memory of this girl.

"Marie Sauvée! *You*—HERE!" I exclaimed in her own tongue.

At the name, now, the whole story, like the bright side of a dark-lantern, flashed. It was a tale of sorrow and shame, as sad, perhaps, as any that it had been my lot to meet. So far as I had ever known, the little French girl, thrown in my way while I was serving in barracks at Washington, had baffled every effort I had made to win her affection or her confidence, and had gone out of my life as the thistle-down flies on the wind. She had cost me many of those precious drops of the soul's blood which all such endeavor drains; and in the laboratory of memory I had labelled them, "Worse than Wasted," and sadly wondered if I should do the same again for such another need, at just such hopeless expenditure, and had reminded myself that it was not good spiritual economy, and said that I would never repeat the experience, and known all the while that I should.

Now here, a spirit saved, shining as the air of Heaven, "without spot or any such thing"—here, wiser in heavenly lore than I, longer with Him than I, nearer to Him than I, dearer to Him, perhaps, than I—*here* was Marie Sauvée.

"I do not know how to apologize," I said, struggling with my emotion, "for the way in which I spoke to you just now. Why should you not be here? Why, indeed? Why am I here? Why"—

"Dear Miss Mary," cried the girl, interrupting me passionately, "but for you it might never have been as it is. Or never for ages—I cannot say. I might have been a ghost, bound yet to the hated ghost of the old life. It was your doing, at the first—down there—all those years ago. Miss Mary, you were the first person I ever loved. You didn't know it. I had no idea of telling you. But I did, I loved you. After you went away, I loved you; ever since then, I loved you. I said, I will be fit to love her before I die. And then I said, I will go where she is going, for I shall never get at her anywhere else. And when I entered this place—for I had no friend or relative here that I knew, to meet me—I was more frightened than it is possible for any one like you to understand, and wondered what place there could be for one like me in all this country, and how I could ever get accustomed to their ways, and whether I should shock and grieve them—you *can't* understand *that*; I dreaded it so, I was afraid I should swear after I got to Heaven; I was afraid I might say some evil word, and shame them all, and shame myself more than I could ever get over. I knew I wasn't educated for any such society. I knew there wasn't anything in me that would be at home here, but just"—

"But just what, Marie?" I asked, with a humility deeper than I could have expressed.

"But just my love for you, Miss Mary. That was all. I had nothing to come to Heaven on, but loving you and meaning to be a better girl because I loved you. That was truly all."

"That is impossible!" I said quickly. "Your love for me never brought you here of itself alone. You are mistaken about this. It is neither Christianity nor philosophy."

"There is no mistake," persisted the girl, with gentle obstinacy, smiling delightedly at my dogmatism, "I came here because I loved you. Do you not see? In loving you, I loved—for the first time in my life I loved—goodness. I really did. And when I got to this place, I found out that goodness was the same as God. And I had been getting the love of God into my heart, all that time, in that strange way, and never knew how it was with me, until—Oh,

Miss Mary, who do you think it was, WHO, that met me within an hour after I died?"

"It was our Master," she added in an awe-struck, yet rapturous whisper, that thrilled me through. "It was He Himself. He was the first, for I had nobody, as I told you, belonging to me in this holy place, to care for a wretch like me.—*He* was the first to meet *me*! And it was He who taught me everything I had to learn. It was He who made me feel acquainted and at home. It was He who took me on from love of you, to love of Him, as you put one foot after another in learning to walk after you have had a terrible sickness. And it was *He* who never reminded me—never once reminded me—of the sinful creature I had been. Never, by one word or look, from that hour to this day, has He let me feel ashamed in Heaven. That is what *He* is!" cried the girl, turning upon me, in a little sudden, sharp way she used to have; her face and form were so transfigured before me, as she spoke, that it seemed as if she quivered with excess of light, and were about to break away and diffuse herself upon the radiant air, like song, or happy speech, or melting color.

"Die for Him!" she said after a passionate silence. "If I could die everlastingly and everlastingly and everlastingly, to give Him any pleasure, or to save Him any pain— But then, that's nothing," she added, "I love Him. That is all that means.—And I've only got to live everlastingly instead. That is the way He has treated me—*me*!"

IX.

THE shore upon which we had landed was thickly populated, as I have said. Through a sweep of surpassingly beautiful suburbs, we approached the streets of a town. It is hard to say why I should have been surprised at finding in this place the signs of human traffic, philanthropy, art, and study—what otherwise I expected, who can say? My impressions, as Marie Sauvée led me through the city, had the confusion of sudden pleasure. The width and shining cleanliness of the streets, the beauty and glittering material of the houses, the frequent presence of libraries, museums, public gardens, signs of attention to the wants of animals, and places of shelter for travelers such as I had never seen in the most advanced and benevolent of cities below,— these were the points that struck me most forcibly.

The next thing, which in a different mood might have been the first that impressed me was the remarkable expression of the faces that I met or passed. No thoughtful person can have failed to observe, in any throng, the preponderant look of unrest and dissatisfaction in the human eye. Nothing, to a fine vision, so emphasizes the isolation of being, as the faces of people in a crowd. In this new community to which I had been brought, that old effect was replaced by a delightful change. I perceived, indeed, great intentness of purpose here, as in all thickly-settled regions; the countenances that passed me indicated close conservation of social force and economy of intellectual energy; these were people trained by attrition with many influences, and balanced with the conflict of various interests. But these were men and women, busy without hurry, efficacious without waste; they had ambition without unscrupulousness, power without tyranny, success without vanity, care without anxiety, effort without exhaustion,—hope, fear, toil, uncertainty it seemed, elation it was sure—but a repose that it was impossible to call by any other name than divine, controlled their movements, which were like the pendulum of a golden clock whose works are out of sight. I watched these people with delight. Great numbers of them seemed to be students, thronging what we should call below colleges, seminaries, or schools of art, or music, or science. The proportion of persons pursuing some form of intellectual acquisition struck me as large. My little guide, to whom I mentioned this, assented to the fact, pointing out to me a certain institution we had passed, at which she herself was, she said, something like a primary scholar, and from which she had been given a holiday to meet me as she did, and conduct me through the journey that had been appointed for me on that day. I inquired of her what her studies might be like; but she told me that she was hardly wise enough as yet to explain to me what I could learn for myself when I had been longer in this place, and when my leisure came for investigating its attractions at my own will.

"I am uncommonly ignorant, you know," said Marie Sauvée humbly, "I have everything to learn. There is book knowledge and thought knowledge and soul knowledge, and I have not any of these. I was as much of what you used to call a heathen, as any Fiji-Islander you gave your missionaries to. I have so much to learn, that I am not sent yet upon other business such as I should like."

Upon my asking Marie Sauvée what business this might be, she hesitated. "I have become ambitious in Heaven," she answered slowly. "I shall never be content till I am fit to be sent to the worst woman that can be found—no matter which side of death—I don't care in what world—I want to be sent to one that nobody else will touch; I think I might know how to save her. It is a tremendous ambition!" she repeated. "Preposterous for the greatest angel there is here! And yet I—*I* mean to do it."

I was led on in this way by Marie Sauvée, through and out of the city into the western suburbs; we had approached from the east, and had walked a long distance. There did not occur to me, I think, till we had made the circuit of the beautiful town, one thing, which, when I did observe it, struck me as, on the whole, the most impressive that I had noticed. "I have not seen," I said, stopping suddenly, "I have not seen a poor person in all this city."

"Nor an aged one, have you?" asked Marie Sauvée, smiling.

"Now that I think of it,—no. Nor a sick one. Not a beggar. Not a cripple. Not a mourner. Not—and yet what have we here? This building, by which you are leading me, bears a device above the door, the last I should ever have expected to find *here*."

It was an imposing building, of a certain translucent material that had the massiveness of marble, with the delicacy of thin agate illuminated from within. The rear of this building gave upon the open country, with a background of hills, and the vision of the sea which I had crossed. People strolled about the grounds, which had more than the magnificence of Oriental gardens. Music came from the building, and the saunterers, whom I saw, seemed nevertheless not to be idlers, but persons busily employed in various ways—I should have said, under the close direction of others who guided them. The inscription above the door of this building was a word, in a tongue unknown to me, meaning "Hospital," as I was told.

"They are the sick at heart," said Marie Sauvée, in answer to my look of perplexity, "who are healed there. And they are the sick of soul; those who were most unready for the new life; they whose spiritual being was diseased through inaction, *they* are the invalids of Heaven. There they are put under treatment, and slowly cured. With some, it takes long. I was there myself when I first came, for a little; it will be a most interesting place for you to visit, by-and-by."

I inquired who were the physicians of this celestial sanitarium.

"They who unite the natural love of healing to the highest spiritual development."

"By no means, then, necessarily they who were skilled in the treatment of diseases on earth?" I asked, laughing.

"Such are oftener among the patients," said Marie Sauvée sadly. To me, so lately from the earth, and our low earthly way of finding amusement in facts of this nature, this girl's gravity was a rebuke. I thanked her for it, and we passed by the hospital—which I secretly made up my mind to investigate at another time—and so out into the wider country, more sparsely settled, but it seemed to me more beautiful than that we had left behind.

"There," I said, at length, "is to my taste the loveliest spot we have seen yet. That is the most homelike of all these homes."

We stopped before a small and quiet house built of curiously inlaid woods, that reminded me of Sorrento work as a great achievement may remind one of a first and faint suggestion. So exquisite was the carving and coloring, that on a larger scale the effect might have interfered with the solidity of the building, but so modest were the proportions of this charming house, that its dignity was only enhanced by its delicacy. It was shielded by trees, some familiar to me, others strange. There were flowers—not too many; birds; and I noticed a fine dog sunning himself upon the steps. The sweep of landscape from all the windows of this house must have been grand. The wind drove up from the sea. The light, which had a peculiar depth and color, reminding me of that which on earth flows from under the edge of a breaking storm-cloud at the hour preceding sunset, formed an aureola about the house. When my companion suggested my examining this place, since it so attracted me, I hesitated, but yielding to her wiser judgment, strolled across the little lawn, and stood, uncertain, at the threshold. The dog arose as I came up, and met me cordially, but no person seemed to be in sight.

"Enter," said Marie Sauvée in a tone of decision. "You are expected. Go where you will."

I turned to remonstrate with her, but the girl had disappeared. Finding myself thus thrown on my own resources, and having learned already the value of obedience to mysterious influences in this new life, I gathered courage, and went into the house. The dog followed me affectionately, rather than suspiciously.

For a few moments I stood in the hall or ante-room, alone and perplexed. Doors opened at right and left, and vistas of exquisitely-ordered rooms stretched out. I saw much of the familiar furniture of a modest home, and much that was unfamiliar mingled therewith. I desired to ask the names or purposes of certain useful articles, and the characters and creators of certain works of art. I was bewildered and delighted. I had something of the feeling of a rustic visitor taken for the first time to a palace or imposing town-house.

Was Heaven an aggregate of homes like this? Did everlasting life move on in the same dear ordered channel—the dearest that human experiment had ever found—the channel of family love? Had one, after death, the old blessedness without the old burden? The old sweetness without the old mistake? The familiar rest, and never the familiar fret? Was there always in the eternal world "somebody to come home to"? And was there always the knowledge that it could not be the wrong person? Was all *that* eliminated from celestial domestic life? Did Heaven solve the problem on which earth had done no more than speculate?

While I stood, gone well astray on thoughts like these, feeling still too great a delicacy about my uninvited presence in this house, I heard the steps of the host, or so I took them to be; they had the indefinable ring of the master's foot. I remained where I was, not without embarrassment, ready to apologize for my intrusion as soon as he should come within sight. He crossed the long room at the left, leisurely; I counted his quiet footsteps; he advanced, turned, saw me—I too, turned—and so, in this way, it came about that I stood face to face with my own father.

... I had found the eternal life full of the unexpected, but this was almost the sweetest thing that had happened to me yet.

Presently my father took me over the house and the grounds; with a boyish delight, explaining to me how many years he had been building and constructing and waiting with patience in his heavenly home for the first one of his own to join him. Now, he too, should have "somebody to come home to." As we dwelt upon the past and glanced at the future, our full hearts overflowed. He explained to me that my new life had but now, in the practical sense of the word, begun; since a human home was the centre of all growth and blessedness. When he had shown me to my own portion of the house, and bidden me welcome to it, he pointed out to me a certain room whose door stood always open, but whose threshold was never crossed. I hardly feel that I have the right, in this public way, to describe, in detail, the construction or adornment of this room. I need only say that Heaven itself seemed to have been ransacked to bring together the daintiest, the most delicate, the purest, thoughts and fancies that celestial skill or art could create. Years had gone to the creation of this spot; it was a growth of time, the occupation of that loneliness which must be even in the happy life, when death has temporarily separated two who had been one. I was quite prepared for his whispered words, when he said,—

"Your mother's room, my dear. It will be all ready for her at any time."

This union had been a *marriage*—not one of the imperfect ties that pass under the name, on earth. Afterwards, when I learned more of the social economy of the new life, I perceived more clearly the rarity and peculiar value of an experience which had in it the elements of what might be called (if I should be allowed the phrase) eternal permanency, and which involved, therefore, none of the disintegration and redistribution of relations consequent upon passing from temporary or mistaken choices to a fixed and perfect state of society.

Later, on that same evening, I was called eagerly from below. I was resting, and alone;—I had, so to speak, drawn my first breath in Heaven; once again, like a girl in my own room under my father's roof; my heart at anchor, and my peace at full tide. I ran as I used to run, years ago, when he called me, crying down,—

"I'm coming, Father," while I delayed a moment to freshen my dress, and to fasten it with some strange white flowers that climbed over my window, and peered, nodding like children, into the room.

When I reached the hall, or whatever might be the celestial name for the entrance room below, I did not immediately see my father, but I heard the sound of voices beyond, and perceived the presence of many people in the house. As I hesitated, wondering what might be the etiquette of these new conditions, and whether I should be expected to play the hostess at a reception of angels or saints, some one came up from behind me, I think, and held out his hand in silence.

"St. Johns!" I cried, "Jamie St. Johns! The last time I saw *you*"—

"The last time you saw me was in a field-hospital after the battle of Malvern Hills," said St. Johns. "I died in your arms, Miss Mary. Shot flew about you while you got me that last cup of water. I died hard. You sang the hymn I asked for—'Ye who tossed on beds of pain'—and the shell struck the tent-pole twenty feet off, but you sang right on. I was afraid you would stop. I was almost gone. But you never faltered. You sang my soul out—do you remember? I've been watching all this while for you. I've been a pretty busy man since I got to this place, but I've always found time to run in and ask your father when he expected you.

"I meant to be the first all along; but I hear there's a girl got ahead of me. She's here, too, and some more women. But most of us are the boys, to-night, Miss Mary,—come to give you a sort of house-warming—just to say we've never forgotten!... and you see we want to say 'Welcome home at last' to *our* army woman—God bless her—as she blessed us!

"Come in, Miss Mary! Don't feel bashful. It's nobody but your own boys. Here we are. There's a thing I remember—you used to read it. '*For when ye fail*'—you know I never could quote straight—'*they shall receive you into everlasting habitations*'—Wasn't that it? Now here. See! Count us! *Not one missing*, do you see? You said you'd have us all here yet—all that died before you did. You used to tell us so. You prayed it, and you lived it, and you did it, and, by His everlasting mercy, here we are. Look us over. Count again. I couldn't make a speech on earth and I can't make one in Heaven—but the fellows put me up to it. *Come* in, Miss Mary! *Dear* Miss Mary—why, we want to shake hands with you, all around! We want to sit and tell army-stories half the night. We want to have some of the old songs, and—What! Crying, Miss Mary?— *You?* We never saw you cry in all our lives. Your lip used to tremble. You got pretty white; but you weren't that kind of woman. Oh, see here! *Crying* in HEAVEN?"—

X.

FROM this time, the events which I am trying to relate began to assume in fact a much more orderly course; yet in form I scarcely find them more easy to present. Narrative, as has been said of conversation, "is always but a selection," and in this case the peculiar difficulties of choosing from an immense mass of material that which can be most fitly compressed into the compass allowed me by these few pages, are so great, that I have again and again laid down my task in despair; only to be urged on by my conviction that it is more clearly my duty to speak what may carry comfort to the hearts of some, than to worry because my imperfect manner of expression may offend the heads of others. All I can presume to hope for this record of an experience is, that it may have a passing value to certain of my readers whose anticipations of what they call "the Hereafter" are so vague or so dubious as to be more of a pain than a pleasure to themselves.

From the time of my reception into my father's house, I lost the sense of homelessness which had more or less possessed me since my entrance upon the new life, and felt myself becoming again a member of an organized society, with definite duties as well as assured pleasures before me.

These duties I did not find astonishingly different in their essence, while they had changed greatly in form, from those which had occupied me upon earth. I found myself still involved in certain filial and domestic responsibilities, in intellectual acquisition, in the moral support of others, and in spiritual self-culture. I found myself a member of an active community in which not a drone nor an invalid could be counted, and I quickly became, like others who surrounded me, an exceedingly busy person. At first my occupations did not assume sharp professional distinctiveness, but had rather the character of such as would belong to one in training for a more cultivated condition. This seemed to be true of many of my fellow-citizens; that they were still in a state of education for superior usefulness or happiness. With others, as I have intimated, it was not so. My father's business, for instance, remained what it had always been—that of a religious teacher; and I met women and men as well, to whom, as in the case of my old neighbor, Mrs. Mersey, there had been set apart an especial fellowship with the spirits of the recently dead or still living, who had need of great guidance. I soon formed, by observation, at least, the acquaintance, too, of a wide variety of natures;— I met artisans and artists, poets and scientists, people of agricultural pursuits, mechanical inventors, musicians, physicians, students, tradesmen, aerial messengers to the earth, or to other planets, and a long list besides, that would puzzle more than it would enlighten, should I attempt to describe it. I mention these points, which I have no space to amplify, mainly to give reality to any allusions that I shall make to my relations in the heavenly city, and to let it be understood that I speak of a community as organized and as various as Paris or New York; which possessed all the advantages and none of the evils that we are accustomed to associate with massed population; that such a community existed without sorrow, without sickness, without death, without anxiety, and without sin; that the evidences of almost incredible harmony, growth, and happiness which I saw before me in that one locality, I had reason to believe extended to uncounted others in unknown regions, thronging with joys and activities the mysteries of space and time.

For reasons which will be made clear as I approach the end of my narrative, I cannot speak as fully of many high and marvelous matters in the eternal life, as I wish that I might have done. I am giving impressions which, I am keenly aware, have almost the imperfection of a broken dream. I can only crave from the reader, on trust, a patience which he may be more ready to grant me at a later time.

I now began, as I say, to assume regular duties and pleasures; among the keenest of the latter was the constant meeting of old friends and acquaintances. Much perplexity, great delight, and some disappointment awaited me in these *dénouements* of earthly story.

The people whom I had naturally expected to meet earliest were often longest delayed from crossing my path; in some cases, they were altogether missing. Again, I was startled by coming in contact with individuals that I had never associated, in my conceptions of the future, with a spiritual existence at all; in these cases I was sometimes humbled by discovering a type of spiritual character so far above my own, that my fancies in their behalf proved to be unwarrantable self-sufficiency. Social life in the heavenly world, I soon learned, was a series of subtle or acute surprises. It sometimes reminded me of a simile of George Eliot's, wherein she likened human existence to a game of chess in which each one of the pieces had intellect and passions, and the player might be beaten by his own pawns. The element of unexpectedness, which constitutes the first and yet the most unreliable charm of earthly society, had here acquired a permanent dignity. One of the most memorable things which I observed about heavenly relations was, that people did not, in the degree or way to which I was accustomed, tire of each other. Attractions, to begin with, were less lightly experienced; their hold was deeper; their consequences more lasting. I had not been under my new conditions long, before I learned that here genuine feeling was never suffered to fall a sacrifice to intellectual curiosity, or emotional caprice; that here one had at last the stimulus of social attrition without its perils, its healthy pleasures without its pains. I learned, of course, much else, which it is more than difficult, and some things which it is impossible, to explain. I testify only of what I am permitted.

Among the intellectual labors that I earliest undertook was the command of the Universal Language, which I soon found necessary to my convenience. In a community like that I had entered, many nationalities were represented, and I observed that while each retained its own familiar earthly tongue, and one had the pleasant opportunity of acquiring as many others as one chose, yet a common vocabulary became a desideratum of which, indeed, no one was compelled to avail himself contrary to his taste, but in which many, like myself, found the greatest pleasure and profit. The command of this language occupied much well-directed time.

I should not omit to say that a portion of my duty and my privilege consisted in renewed visits to the dearly-loved whom I had left upon the earth. These visits were sometimes matters of will with me. Again, they were strictly occasions of permission, and again, I was denied the power to make them when I most deeply desired to do so. Herein I learned the difference between trial and trouble, and that while the last was stricken out of heavenly life, the first distinctly remained. It is pleasant to me to remember that I was allowed to be of more than a little comfort to those who mourned for me; that it was I who guided them from despair to endurance, and so through peace to cheerfulness, and the hearty renewal of daily human content. These visits were for a long time—excepting the rare occasions on which I met Him who had spoken to me upon the sea-shore—the deepest delight which was offered me.

Upon one point I foresee that I shall be questioned by those who have had the patience so far to follow my recital. What, it will be asked, was the political constitution of the community you describe? What place in celestial society has worldly caste?

When I say, strictly none at all, let me not be misunderstood. I observed the greatest varieties of rank in the celestial kingdom, which seemed to me rather a close Theocracy than a wild commune. There were powers above me, and powers below; there were natural and harmonious social selections; there were laws and their officers; there was obedience and its dignity; there was influence and its authority; there were gifts and their distinctions. I may say that I found far more reverence for differences of rank or influence than I was used to seeing, at least in my own corner of the earth. The main point was that the basis of the whole thing had undergone a tremendous change. Inheritance, wealth, intellect, genius, beauty, all the old passports to power, were replaced by one so simple yet so autocratic, that I hardly know how to give any idea at once of its dignity and its sweetness. I may call this personal holiness. Position, in the new life, I found depended upon spiritual claims. Distinction was the result of character. The nature nearest to the Divine Nature ruled the social forces. Spiritual culture was the ultimate test of individual importance.

I inquired one day for a certain writer of world-wide—I mean of earth-wide—celebrity, who, I had learned, was a temporary visitor in the city, and whom I wished to meet. I will not for sufficient reasons mention the name of this man, who had been called the genius of his century, below. I had anticipated that a great ovation would be given him, in which I desired to join, and I was surprised that his presence made little or no stir in our community. Upon investigating the facts, I learned that his public influence was, so far, but a slight one, though it had gradually gained, and was likely to increase with time. He had been a man whose splendid powers were dedicated to the temporary and worldly aspects of Truth, whose private life was selfish and cruel, who had written the most famous poem of his age, but "by all his searching" had not found out God.

In the conditions of the eternal life, this genius had been obliged to set itself to learning the alphabet of spiritual truth; he was still a pupil, rather than a master among us, and I was told that he himself ardently objected to receiving a deference which was not as yet his due; having set the might of his great nature as strenuously now to the spiritual, as once to the intellectual task; in which, I must say, I was not without expectation that he would ultimately outvie us all.

On the same day when this distinguished man entered and left our city (having quietly accomplished his errand), I heard the confusion of some public excitement at a distance, and hastening to see what it meant, I discovered that the object of it was a plain, I thought in her earthly life she must have been a poor woman, obscure, perhaps, and timid. The people pressed towards her, and received her into the town by acclamation. They crowned her with amaranth and flung lilies in her path. The authorities of the city officially met her; the people of influence hastened to beseech her to do honor to their homes by her modest presence; we crowded for a sight of her, we begged for a word from her, we bewildered her with our tributes, till she hid her blushing face and was swept out of our sight.

"But who is this," I asked an eager passer, "to whom such an extraordinary reception is tendered? I have seen nothing like it since I came here."

"Is it possible you do not know —— ——?"

My informant gave a name which indeed was not unfamiliar to me; it was that of a woman who had united to extreme beauty of private character, and a high type of faith in invisible truths, life-long devotion to an unpopular philanthropy. She had never been called a "great" woman on earth. Her influence had not been large. Her cause had never been the fashion, while she herself was living. Society had never amused itself by adopting her, even to the extent of a parlor lecture. Her name, so far as it was familiar to the public at all, had been the synonym of a poor zealot, a plain fanatic, to be tolerated for her conscientiousness and—avoided for her earnestness. Since her death, the humane consecration which she represented had marched on like a conquering army over her grave. Earth, of which she was not worthy, had known her too late. Heaven was proud to do honor to the spiritual foresight and sustained self-denial, as royal as it was rare.

I remember, also, being deeply touched by a sight upon which I chanced, one morning, when I was strolling about the suburbs of the city, seeking the refreshment of solitude before the duties of the day began. For, while I was thus engaged, I met our Master, suddenly. He was busily occupied with others, and, beyond the deep recognition of His smile, I had no converse with Him. He was followed at a little distance, as He was apt to be, by a group of playing children; but He was in close communion with two whom I saw to be souls newly-arrived from the lower life. One of these was a man—I should say he had been a rough man, and had come out of a rude life—who conversed with Him eagerly but reverently, as they walked on towards the town. Upon the other side, our Lord held with His own hand the hand of a timid, trembling woman, who scarcely dared raise her eyes from the ground; now and then she drew His garment's edge furtively to her lips, and let it fall again, with the slow motion of one who is in a dream of ecstasy. These two people, I judged, had no connection with each other beyond the fact that they were simultaneous new-comers to the new country, and had, perhaps, both borne with them either special need or merit, I could hardly decide which. I took occasion to ask a neighbor, an old resident of the city, and wise in its mysteries, what he supposed to be the explanation of the scene before us, and why these two were so distinguished by the favor of Him whose least glance made holiday in the soul of any one of us. It was then explained to me, that the man about whom I had inquired was the hero of a great calamity, with which the lower world was at present occupied. One of the most frightful railway accidents of this generation had been averted, and the lives of four hundred helpless passengers saved, by the sublime sacrifice of this locomotive engineer, who died (it will be remembered) a death of voluntary and unique torture to save his train. All that could be said of the tragedy was that it held the essence of self-sacrifice in a form seldom attained by man. At the moment I saw this noble fellow, he had so immediately come among us that the expression of physical agony had hardly yet died out of his face, and his eye still blazed with the fire of his tremendous deed.

"But who is the woman?" I asked.

"She was a delicate creature—sick—died of the fright and shock; the only passenger on the train who did not escape."

I inquired why she too was thus preferred; what glorious deed had she done, to make her so dear to the Divine Heart?

"She? Ah, she," said my informant, "was only one of the household saints. She had been notable among celestial observers for many years. You know the type I mean—shy, silent—never thinks of herself, scarcely knows she has a self—toils, drudges, endures, prays; expects nothing of her friends, and gives all; hopes for little, even from her Lord, but surrenders everything; full of religious ideals, not all of them theoretically wise, but practically noble; a woman ready to be cut to inch pieces for her faith in an invisible Love that has never apparently given her anything in particular. Oh, you know the kind of woman: has never had anything of her own, in all her life—not even her own room—and a whole family adore her without knowing it, and lean upon her like infants without seeing it. We have been watching for this woman's coming. We knew there would be an especial greeting for her. But nobody thought of her accompanying the engineer. Come! Shall we not follow, and see how they will be received? If I am not mistaken, it will be a great day in the city."

XI.

AMONG the inquiries that must be raised by my fragmentary recital, I am only too keenly aware of the difficulty of answering one which I do not see my way altogether to ignore. I refer to that affecting the domestic relations of the eternal world.

It will be readily seen that I might not be permitted to share much of the results of my observation in this direction, with earthly curiosity, or even earthly anxiety. It is not without thought and prayer for close guidance that I suffer myself to say, in as few words as possible, that I found the unions which go to form heavenly homes so different from the marriage relations of earth, in their laws of selection and government, that I quickly understood the meaning of our Lord's few revealed words as to that matter; while yet I do not find myself at liberty to explain either the words or the facts. I think I cannot be wrong in adding, that in a number of cases, so great as to astonish me, the marriages of earth had no historic effect upon the ties of Heaven. Laws of affiliation uniting soul to soul in a relation infinitely closer than a bond, and more permanent than any which the average human experience would lead to if it were socially a free agent, controlled the attractions of this pure and happy life, in a manner of which I can only say that it must remain a mystery to the earthly imagination. I have intimated that in some cases the choices of time were so blessed as to become the choices of Eternity. I may say, that if I found it lawful to utter the impulse of my soul, I should cry throughout the breadth of the earth a warning to the lightness, or the haste, or the presumption, or the mistake that chose to love for one world, when it might have loved for two.

For, let me say most solemnly, that the relations made between man and woman on earth I found to be, in importance to the individual, second to nothing in the range of human experience, save the adjustment of the soul to the Personality of God Himself.

If I say that I found earthly marriage to have been a temporary expedient for preserving the form of the eternal fact; that freedom in this as in all other things became in Heaven the highest law; that the great sea of human misery, swelled by the passion of love on earth, shall evaporate to the last drop in the blaze of bliss to which no human counterpart can approach any nearer than a shadow to the sun,—I may be understood by those for whose sake alone it is worth while to allude to this mystery at all; for the rest it matters little.

Perhaps I should say, once for all, that every form of pure pleasure or happiness which had existed upon the earth had existed as a type of a greater. Our divinest hours below had been scarcely more than suggestions of their counterparts above. I do not expect to be understood. It must only be remembered that, in all instances, the celestial life develops the soul of a thing. When I speak of eating and drinking, for instance, I do not mean that we cooked and prepared our food as we do below. The elements of nutrition continued to exist for us as they had in the earth, the air, the water, though they were available without drudgery or anxiety. Yet I mean distinctly that the sense of taste remained, that it was gratified at need, that it was a finer one and gave a keener pleasure than its coarser prototype below. I mean that the *soul of a sense* is a more exquisite thing than what we may call the body of the sense, as developed to earthly consciousness.

So far from there being any diminution in the number or power of the senses in the spiritual life, I found not only an acuter intensity in those which we already possessed, but that the effect of our new conditions was to create others of whose character we had never dreamed. To be sure, wise men had forecast the possibility of this fact, differing among themselves even as to the accepted classification of what they had, as Scaliger who called speech the sixth sense, or our English contemporary who included heat and force in his list (also of six); or more imaginative men who had admitted the conceivability of inconceivable powers in an order of being beyond the human. Knowing a little of these speculations, I was not so much surprised at the facts as overwhelmed by their extent and variety. Yet if I try to explain them, I am met by an almost insurmountable obstacle.

It is well known that missionaries are often thwarted in their religious labors by the absence in savage tongues of any words corresponding to certain ideas such as that of purity or unselfishness. Philologists have told us of one African tribe in whose language exist six different words descriptive of murder; none whatever expressive of love. In another no such word as gratitude can be found. Perhaps no illustration can better serve to indicate the impediments which bar the way to my describing to beings who possess but five senses and their corresponding imaginative culture, the habits or enjoyments consequent upon the development of ten senses or fifteen. I am allowed to say as much as this: that the growth of these celestial powers was variable with individuals throughout the higher world, or so much of it as I became acquainted with. It will be readily seen what an illimitable scope for anticipation or achievement is given to daily life by such an evolution of the nature. It should be carefully remembered that this serves only as a single instance of the exuberance of what we call everlasting life.

Below, I remember that I used sometimes to doubt the possibility of one's being happy forever under any conditions, and had moods in which I used to question the value of endless existence. I wish most earnestly to say, that before I had been in Heaven days, Eternity did not seem long enough to make room for the growth of character, the growth of mind, the variety of enjoyment and employment, and the increase of usefulness that practically constituted immortality.

It could not have been long after my arrival at my father's house that he took me with him to the great music hall of our city. It was my first attendance at any one of the public festivals of these happy people, and one long to be treasured in thought. It was, in fact, nothing less than the occasion of a visit by Beethoven, and the performance of a new oratorio of his own, which he conducted in person. Long before the opening hour the streets of the city were thronged. People with holiday expressions poured in from the country. It was a gala-day with all the young folks especially, much as such matters go below. A beautiful thing which I noticed was the absence of all personal insistence in the crowd. The weakest, or the saddest, or the most timid, or those who, for any reason, had the more need of this great pleasure, were selected by their neighbors and urged on into the more desirable positions. The music hall, so-called, was situated upon a hill just outside the town, and consisted of an immense roof supported by rose-colored marble pillars. There were no walls to the building, so that there was the effect of being no limit to the audience, which extended past the line of luxuriously covered seats provided for them, upon the grass, and even into the streets leading to the city. So perfect were what we should call below the telephonic arrangement of the community, that those who remained in their own homes or pursued their usual avocations were not deprived of the music. My impressions are that every person in the city, who desired to put himself in communication with it, heard the oratorio; but I am not familiar with the system by which this was effected. It involved a high advance in the study of acoustics, and was one of the things which I noted to be studied at a wiser time.

Many distinguished persons known to you below, were present, some from our own neighborhood, and others guests of the city. It was delightful to observe the absence of all jealousy or narrow criticism among themselves, and also the reverence with which their superiority was regarded by the less gifted. Every good or great thing seemed to be so heartily shared with every being capable of sharing it, and all personal gifts to become material for such universal pride, that one experienced a kind of transport at the elevation of the public character.

I remembered how it used to be below, when I was present at some musical festival in the familiar hall where the bronze statue of Beethoven, behind the sea of sound, stood calmly. How he towered above our poor unfinished story! As we grouped there, sitting each isolated with his own thirst, brought to be slaked or excited by the flood of music; drinking down into our frivolity or our despair the outlet of that mighty life, it used to seem to me that I heard, far above the passion of the orchestra, his own high words,—his own music made articulate,—"*I go to meet Death with joy.*"

When there came upon the people in that heavenly audience-room a stir, like the rustling of a dead leaf upon crusted snow; when the stir grew to a solemn murmur; when the murmur ran into a lofty cry; when I saw that the orchestra, the chorus, and the audience had risen like one breathless man, and knew that Beethoven stood before us, the light of day darkened for that instant before me. The prelude was well under way, I think, before I dared lift my eyes to his face.

The great tide swept me on. When upon earth had he created sound like this? Where upon earth had we heard its like? There he is, one listening nerve from head to foot, he who used to stand deaf in the middle of his own orchestra—desolate no more, denied no more forever, all the heavenly senses possible to Beethoven awake to the last delicate response; all the solemn faith in the invisible, in the holy, which he had made his own, triumphant now; all the powers of his mighty nature in action like a rising storm—there stands Beethoven immortally alive.

What knew we of music, I say, who heard its earthly prototype? It was but the tuning of the instruments before the eternal orchestra shall sound. Soul! swing yourself free upon this mighty current. Of what will Beethoven tell us whom he dashes on like drops?

As the pæan rises, I bow my life to understand. What would he with us whom God chose to make Beethoven everlastingly? What is the burden of this master's message, given now in Heaven, as once on earth? Do we hear aright? Do we read the score correctly?

"Holy—holy"—

A chorus of angel voices, trained since the time when morning stars sang together with the sons of God, take up the words:

"Holy, *holy*, HOLY is the Lord.". . . . .

When the oratorio has ended, and we glide out, each hushed as a hidden thought, to his own ways, I stay beneath a linden-tree to gather breath. A fine sound, faint as the music of a dream, strikes my ringing ears, and, looking up, I see that the leaf above my head is singing. Has it, too, been one of the great chorus yonder? Did he command the forces of nature, as he did the seraphs of Heaven, or the powers of earth?

The strain falls away slowly from the lips of the leaf:

"Holy, holy, holy,"—

It trembles, and is still.

XII.

THAT which it is permitted me to relate to you moves on swiftly before the thoughts, like the compression in the last act of a drama. The next scene which starts from the variousness of heavenly delight I find to be the Symphony of Color.

There was a time in the history of art, below, when this, and similar phrases, had acquired almost a slang significance, owing to the affectation of their use by the shallow. I was, therefore, the more surprised at meeting a fact so lofty behind the guise of the familiar words; and noted it as but one of many instances in which the earthly had deteriorated from the ideals of the celestial life.

It seemed that the development of color had reached a point never conceived of below, and that the treatment of it constituted an art by itself. By this I do not mean its treatment under the form of painting, decoration, dress, or any embodiment whatever. What we were called to witness was an exhibition of color, pure and simple.

This occasion, of which I especially speak, was controlled by great colorists, some of earthly, some of heavenly renown. Not all of them were artists in the accepted sense of designers; among them were one or two select creatures in whom the passion of color had been remarkable, but, so far as the lower world was concerned, for the great part inactive, for want of any scientific means of expression.

We have all known the *color natures*, and, if we have had a fine sympathy, have compassionated them as much as any upon earth, whether they were found among the disappointed disciples of Art itself, or hidden away in plain homes, where the paucity of existence held all the delicacy and the dream of life close prisoners.

Among the managers of this Symphony I should say that I observed, at a distance, the form of Raphael. I heard it rumored that Leonardo was present, but I did not see him. There was another celebrated artist engaged in the work, whose name I am not allowed to give. It was an unusual occasion, and had attracted attention at a distance. The Symphony did not take place in our own city, but in an adjacent town, to which our citizens, as well as those of other places, repaired in great numbers. We sat, I remember, in a luxurious coliseum, closely darkened. The building was circular in form; it was indeed a perfect globe, in whose centre, without touching anywhere the superficies, we were seated. Air without light entered freely, I know not how, and fanned our faces perpetually. Distant music appealed to the ear, without engaging it. Pleasures, which we could receive or dismiss at will, wandered by, and were assimilated by those extra senses which I have no means of describing. Whatever could be done to put soul and body in a state of ease so perfect as to admit of complete receptivity, and in a mood so high as to induce the loftiest interpretation of the purely æsthetic entertainment before us, was done in the amazing manner characteristic of this country. I do not know that I had ever felt so keenly as on this occasion the delight taken by God in providing happiness for the children of His discipline and love. We had suffered so much, some of us, below, that it did not seem natural, at first, to accept sheer pleasure as an end in and of itself. But I learned that this, like many other fables in Heaven, had no moral. Live! Be! Do! Be glad! Because He lives, ye live also. Grow! Gain! Achieve! Hope! *That* is to glorify Him and enjoy Him forever. Having fought—rest. Having trusted—know. Having endured—enjoy. Being safe—venture. Being pure—fear not to be sensitive. Being in harmony with the Soul of all delights—dare to indulge thine own soul to the brim therein. Having acquired holiness—thou hast no longer any broken law to fear. Dare to be happy. This was the spirit of daily life among us. "Nothing was required of us but to be natural," as I have said before. And it "was natural to be right," thank God, at last.

Being a new-comer, and still so unlearned, I could not understand the Color Symphony as many of the spectators did, while yet I enjoyed it intensely, as an untaught musical organization may enjoy the most complicated composition. I think it was one of the most stimulating sights I ever saw, and my ambition to master this new art flashed fire at once.

Slowly, as we sat silent, at the centre of that great white globe—it was built of porphyry, I think, or some similar substance—there began to breathe upon the surface pure light. This trembled and deepened, till we were enclosed in a sphere of white fire. This I perceived, to scholars in the science of color, signified distinct thought, as a grand chord does to the musician. Thus it was with the hundred effects which followed. White light quivered into pale blue. Blue struggled with violet. Gold and orange parted. Green and gray and crimson glided on. Rose—the living rose—blushed upon us, and faltered under—over—yonder, till we were shut into a world of it, palpitating. It was as if we had gone behind the soul of a woman's blush, or the meaning of a sunrise. Whoever has known the passion for that color will understand why some of the spectators were with difficulty restrained from flinging themselves down into it, as into a sea of rapture.

There were others more affected by the purple, and even by the scarlet; some, again, by the delicate tints in which was the color of the sun, and by colors which were hints rather than expressions. Marvelous modifications of rays set in. They had their laws, their chords, their harmonies, their scales; they carried their melodies and "execution;" they had themes and ornamentation. Each combination had its meaning. The trained eye received it, as the trained ear receives orchestra or oratory. The senses melted, but the intellect was astir. A perfect composition of color unto color was before us, exquisite in detail, magnificent in mass. Now it seemed as if we ourselves, sitting there ensphered in color, flew around the globe with the quivering rays. Now as if we sank into endless sleep with reposing tints; now as if we drank of color; then as if we dreamed it; now as if we felt it—clasped it; then as if we heard it. We were taken into the heart of it; into the mystery of the June sky, and the grass-blade, the blue-bell, the child's cheek, the cloud at sunset, the snowdrift at twilight. The apple-blossom told us its secret, and the down on the pigeon's neck, and the plume of the rose-curlew, and the robin's-egg, and the hair of blonde women, and the scarlet passion-flower, and the mist over everglades, and the power of a dark eye.

It may be remembered that I have alluded once to the rainbow which I saw soon after reaching the new life, and that I raised a question at the time as to the number of rays exhibited in the celestial prism. As I watched the Symphony, I became convinced that the variety of colors unquestionably far exceeded those with which we were familiar on earth. The Indian occultists indeed had long urged that they saw fourteen tints in the prism; this was the dream of the mystic, who, by a tremendous system of education, claims to have subjected the body to the soul, so that the ordinary laws of nature yield to his control. Physicists had also taught us that the laws of optics involved the necessity of other colors beyond those whose rays were admissible by our present vision; this was the assertion of that science which is indebted more largely to the imagination than the worshiper of the Fact has yet arisen from his prone posture high enough to see.

Now, indeed, I had the truth before me. Colors which no artist's palette, no poet's rapture knew, played upon optic nerves exquisitely trained to receive such effects, and were appropriated by other senses empowered to share them in a manner which human language supplies me with no verb or adjective to express.

As we journeyed home after the Symphony, I was surprised to find how calming had been the effect of its intense excitement. Without fever of pulse or rebel fancy or wearied nerve, I looked about upon the peaceful country. I felt ready for any duty. I was strong for all deprivation. I longed to live more purely. I prayed to live more unselfishly. I greatly wished to share the pleasure, with which I had been blessed, with some denied soul. I thought of uneducated people, and coarse people, who had yet to be trained to so many of the highest varieties of happiness. I thought of sick people, all their earthly lives invalids, recently dead, and now free to live. I wished that I had sought some of these out, and taken them with me to the Symphony.

It was a rare evening, even in the blessed land. I enjoyed the change of scene as I used to do in traveling, below. It was delightful to look abroad and see everywhere prosperity and peace. The children were shouting and tumbling in the fields. Young people strolled laughing by twos or in groups. The vigorous men and women busied themselves or rested at the doors of cosy homes. The ineffable landscape of hill and water stretched on behind the human foreground. Nowhere a chill or a blot; nowhere a tear or a scowl, a deformity, a disability, or an evil passion. There was no flaw in the picture. There was no error in the fact. I felt that I was among a perfectly happy people. I said, "I am in a holy world."

The next day was a Holy Day; we of the earth still called it the Sabbath, from long habit. I remember an especial excitement on that Holy Day following the Color Symphony, inasmuch as we assembled to be instructed by one whom, above all other men that had ever lived on earth, I should have taken most trouble to hear. This was no other than St. John the Apostle.

I remember that we held the service in the open air, in the fields beyond the city, for "there was no Temple therein." The Beloved Disciple stood above us, on the rising ground. It would be impossible to forget, but it is well-nigh impossible to describe, the appearance of the preacher. I think he had the most sensitive face I ever saw in any man; yet his dignity was unapproachable. He had a ringing voice of remarkable sweetness, and great power of address. He seemed more divested of himself than any orator I had heard. He poured his personality out upon us, like one of the forces of nature, as largely, and as unconsciously.

He taught us much. He reasoned of mysteries over which we had pored helplessly all our lives below. He explained intricate points in the plan of human life. He touched upon the perplexities of religious faith. He cast a great light backward over the long, dim way by which we had crept to our present blessedness. He spoke to us of our deadliest doubts. He confirmed for us our patient belief. He made us ashamed of our distrust and our restlessness. He left us eager for faith. He gave vigor to our spiritual ideals. He spoke to us of the love of God, as the light speaks of the sun. He revealed to us how we had misunderstood Him. Our souls cried out within us, as we remembered our errors. We gathered ourselves like soldiers as we knew our possibilities. We swayed in his hands as the bough sways in the wind. Each man looked at his neighbor as one whose eyes ask: "Have I wronged thee? Let me atone." "Can I serve thee? Show me how." All our spiritual life arose like an athlete, to exercise itself; we sought hard tasks; we aspired for far prizes; we turned to our daily lives like new-created beings; so truly we had kept Holy Day. When the discourse was over, there followed an anthem sung by a choir of child-angels hovering in mid-air above the preacher, and beautiful exceedingly to the sight and to the ear. "God," they sang, "is

Love—*is* Love—is LOVE." In the refrain we joined with our own awed voices.

The chant died away. All the air of all the worlds was still. The beloved Disciple raised his hand in solemn signal. A majestic Form glided to his side. To whom should the fisherman of Galilee turn with a look like *that?* Oh, grace of God! what a smile was there! The Master and Disciple stand together; they rise above us. See! He falls upon his knees before that Other. So we also, sinking to our own, hide our very faces from the sight.

Our Lord steps forth, and stands alone. To us in glory, as to them of old in sorrow, He is the God made manifest. We do not lift our bowed heads, but we feel that He has raised His piercéd hands above us, and that His own lips call down the Benediction of His Father upon our eternal lives.

XIII.

My father had been absent from home a great deal, taking journeys with whose object he did not acquaint me. I myself had not visited the earth for some time; I cannot say how long. I do not find it possible to divide heavenly time by an earthly calendar, and cannot even decide how much of an interval, by human estimates, had been indeed covered by my residence in the Happy Country, as described upon these pages.

My duties had called me in other directions, and I had been exceedingly busy. My father sometimes spoke of our dear hearts at home, and reported them as all well; but he was not communicative about them. I observed that he took more pains than usual, or I should say more pleasure than usual, in the little domestic cares of our heavenly home. Never had it been in more perfect condition. The garden and the grounds were looking exquisitely. All the trifling comforts or ornaments of the house were to his mind. We talked of them much, and wandered about in our leisure moments, altering or approving details. I did my best to make him happy, but my own heart told me how lonely he must be despite me. We talked less of her coming than we used to do. I felt that he had accepted the separation with the unquestioning spirit which one gains so deeply in Heaven; and that he was content, as one who trusted, still to wait.

One evening, I came home slowly and alone. My father had been away for some days. I had been passing several hours with some friends, who, with myself, had been greatly interested in an event of public importance. A messenger was needed to carry certain tidings to a great astronomer, known to us of old on earth, who was at that time busied in research in a distant planet. It was a desirable embassy, and many sought the opportunity for travel and culture which it gave. After some delay in the appointment, it was given to a person but just arrived from below: a woman not two days dead. This surprised me till I had inquired into the circumstances, when I learned that the new-comer had been on earth an extreme sufferer, bed-ridden for forty years. Much of this time she had been unable even to look out of doors. The airs of Heaven had been shut from her darkened chamber. For years she had not been able to sustain conversation with her own friends, except on rare occasions. Possessed of a fine mind, she had been unable to read, or even to bear the human voice in reading. Acute pain had tortured her days. Sleeplessness had made horror of her nights. She was poor. She was dependent. She was of a refined organization. She was of a high spirit, and of energetic temperament. Medical science, holding out no cure, assured her that she might live to old age. She lived. When she was seventy-six years old, death remembered her. This woman had sometimes been inquired of, touching her faith in that Mystery which we call God. I was told that she gave but one answer; beyond this, revealing no more of experience than the grave itself, to which, more than to any other simile, her life could be likened.

"Though He slay me," she said, "I will trust."

"But, do you never doubt?"

"I *will* trust."

To this rare spirit, set free at last and re-embodied, the commission of which I have spoken was delegated; no one in all the city grudged her its coveted advantages. A mighty shout rose in the public ways when the selection was made known. I should have thought she might become delirious with the sudden access of her freedom, but it was said that she received her fortune quietly, and, slipping out of sight, was away upon her errand before we saw her face.

The incident struck me as a most impressive one, and I was occupied with it, as I walked home thoughtfully. Indeed, I was so absorbed that I went with my eyes cast down, and scarcely noticed when I had reached our own home. I did not glance at the house, but continued my way up the winding walk between the trees, still drowned in my reverie.

It was a most peaceful evening. I felt about me the fine light at which I did not look; that evening glow was one of the new colors,—one of the heavenly colors that I find it impossible to depict. The dog came to meet me as usual; he seemed keenly excited, and would have hurried me into the house. I patted him absently as I strolled on.

Entering the house with a little of the sense of loss which, even in the Happy World, accompanies the absence of those we love, and wondering when my father would be once more with me, I was startled at hearing his voice—no, voices; there were two; they came from an upper chamber, and the silent house echoed gently with their subdued words.

I stood for a moment listening below; I felt the color flash out of my face; my heart stood still. I took a step or two forward—hesitated—advanced with something like fear. The dog pushed before me, and urged me to follow. After a moment's thought I did so, resolutely.

The doors stood open everywhere, and the evening air blew in with a strong and wholesome force. No one had heard me. Guided by the voices of the unseen speakers I hurried on, across the hall, through my own room, and into that sacred spot I have spoken of, wherein for so many solitary years my dear father had made ready for her coming who was the joy of his joy, in Heaven, as she had been on earth.

For that instant, I saw all the familiar details of the room in a blur of light. It was as if a sea of glory filled the place. Across it, out beyond the window, on the balcony which overlooked the hill-country and the sea, stood my father and my mother, hand in hand.

She did not hear me, even yet. They were talking quietly, and were absorbed. Uncertain what to do, I might even have turned and left them undisturbed, so sacred seemed that hour of theirs to me; so separate in all the range of experience in either world, or any life. But her heart warned her, and she stirred, and so saw me—my dear mother—come to us, at last.

Oh, what arms can gather like a mother's, whether in earth or Heaven? Whose else could be those brooding touches, those raining tears, those half-inarticulate maternal words? And for her, too, the bitterness is passed, the blessedness begun. Oh, my dear mother! My dear mother! I thank God I was the child appointed to give you welcome—thus....

"And how is it with Tom,—poor Tom!"

"He has grown such a fine fellow; you cannot think. I leaned upon him. He was the comfort of my old age."

"Poor Tom!"

"And promises to make such a man, dear! A good boy. No bad habits, yet. Your father is so pleased that he makes a scholar."

"Dear Tom! And Alice?"

"It was hard to leave Alice. But she is young. Life is before her. God is good."

"And you, my dearest, was it hard for you at the last? Was it a long sickness? Who took care of you? Mother! did you suffer *much*?"

"Dear, I never suffered any. I had a sudden stroke I think. I was sitting by the fire with the children. It was vacation and Tom was at home. They were all at home. I started to cross the room, and it grew dark. I did not know that I was dead till I found I was standing there upon the balcony, in your father's arms."

"I had to tell her what had happened. She wouldn't believe me at the first."

"Were you with her all the time below?"

"All the time; for days before the end."

"And you brought her here yourself, easily?"

"All the way, myself. She slept like a baby, and wakened—as she says."

XIV.

BUT was it possible to feel desolate in Heaven? Life now filled to the horizon. Our business, our studies, and our pleasures occupied every moment. Every day new expedients of delight unfurled before us. Our conceptions of happiness increased faster than their realization. The imagination itself grew, as much as the aspiration. We saw height beyond height of joy, as we saw outline above outline of duty. How paltry looked our wildest earthly dream! How small our largest worldly deed! One would not have thought it possible that one could even want so much as one demanded here; or hope so far as one expected now.

What possibilities stretched on; each leading to a larger, like newly-discovered stars, one beyond another; as the pleasure or the achievement took its place, the capacity for the next increased. Satiety or its synonyms passed out of our language, except as a reminiscence of the past. See, what were the conditions of this eternal problem. Given: a pure heart, perfect health, unlimited opportunity for usefulness, infinite chance of culture, home, friendship, love; the elimination from practical life of anxiety and separation; and the intense spiritual stimulus of the presence of our dear Master, through whom we approached the mystery of God—how incredible to anything short of experience the sum of happiness!

I soon learned how large a part of our delight consisted in anticipation; since now we knew anticipation without alloy of fear. I thought much of the joys in store for me, which yet I was not perfected enough to attain. I looked onward to the perpetual meeting of old friends and acquaintances, both of the living and the dead; to the command of unknown languages, arts, and sciences, and knowledges manifold; to the grandeur of helping the weak, and revering the strong; to the privilege of guarding the erring or the tried, whether of earth or heaven, and of sharing all attainable wisdom with the less wise, and of even instructing those too ignorant to know that they were not wise, and of ministering to the dying, and of assisting in bringing together the separated. I looked forward to meeting select natures, the distinguished of earth or Heaven; to reading history backward by contact with its actors, and settling its knotty points by their evidential testimony. Was I not in a world where Loyola, and Jeanne d'Arc, or Luther, or Arthur, could be asked questions?

I would follow the experiments of great discoverers, since their advent to this place. What did Newton, and Columbus, and Darwin in the eternal life?

I would keep pace with the development of art. To what standard had Michael Angelo been raising the public taste all these years?

I would join the fragments of those private histories which had long been matter of public interest. Where, and whose now, was Vittoria Colonna?

I would have the *finales* of the old Sacred stories. What use had been made of the impetuosity of Peter? What was the private life of Saint John? With what was the fine intellect of Paul now occupied? What was the charm in the Magdalene? In what sacred fields did the sweet nature of Ruth go gleaning? Did David write the new anthems for the celestial chorals? What was the attitude of Moses towards the Persistence of Force? Where was Judas? And did the Betrayed plead for the betrayer?

I would study the sociology of this explanatory life. Where, if anywhere, were the Cave-men? In what world, and under what educators, were the immortal souls of Laps and Bushmen trained? What social position had the early Christian martyrs? What became of Caligula, whose nurse, we were told, smeared her breasts with blood, and so developed the world-hated tyrant from the outraged infant? Where was Buddha, "the Man who knew"? What affectionate relation subsisted between him and the Man who Loved?

I would bide my time patiently, but I, too, would become an experienced traveler through the spheres. Our Sun I would visit, and scarlet Mars, said by our astronomers below to be the planet most likely to contain inhabitants. The colored suns I would observe, and the nebulæ, and the mysteries of space, powerless now to chill one by its reputed temperature, said to be forever at zero. Where were the Alps of Heaven? The Niagara of celestial scenery? The tropics of the spiritual world? Ah, how I should pursue Eternity with questions!

What was the relation of mechanical power to celestial conditions? What use was made of Watts and Stevenson?

What occupied the ex-hod-carriers and cooks?

Where were all the songs of all the poets? In the eternal accumulation of knowledge, what proportion sifted through the strainers of spiritual criticism? What *were* the standards of spiritual criticism? What became of those creations of the human intellect which had acquired immortality? Were there instances where these figments of fancy had achieved an eternal existence lost by their own creators? Might not one of the possible mysteries of our new state of existence be the fact of a world peopled by the great creatures of our imagination known to us below? And might not one of our pleasures consist in visiting such a world? Was it incredible that Helen, and Lancelot, and Sigfried, and Juliet, and Faust, and Dinah Morris, and the Lady of Shalott, and Don Quixote, and Colonel Newcome, and Sam Weller, and Uncle Tom, and Hester Prynne and Jean Valjean existed? could be approached by way of holiday, as one used to take up the drama or the fiction, on a leisure hour, down below?

Already, though so short a time had I been in the upper life, my imagination was overwhelmed with the sense of its possibilities. They seemed to overlap one another like the molecules of gold in a ring, without visible juncture or practical end. I was ready for the inconceivable itself. In how many worlds should I experience myself? How many lives should I live? Did eternal existence mean eternal variety of growth, suspension, renewal? Might youth and maturity succeed each other exquisitely? Might individual life reproduce itself from seed, to flower, to fruit, like a plant, through the cycles? Would childhood or age be a matter of personal choice? Would the affectional or the intellectual temperaments at will succeed each other? Might one try the domestic or the public career in different existences? Try the bliss of love in one age, the culture of solitude in another? Be oneself yet be all selves? Experience all glories, all discipline, all knowledge, all hope? Know the ecstasy of assured union with the one creature chosen out of time and Eternity to complement the soul? And yet forever pursue the unattainable with the rapture and the reverence of newly-awakened and still ungratified feeling?

Ah me! was it possible to feel desolate even in Heaven?

I think it may be, because I had been much occupied with thoughts like these; or it may be that, since my dear mother's coming, I had been, naturally, thrown more by myself in my desire to leave those two uninterrupted in their first reunion—but I must admit that I had lonely moments, when I realized that Heaven had yet failed to provide me with a home of my own, and that the most loving filial position could not satisfy the nature of a mature man or woman in any world. I must admit that I began to be again subject to retrospects and sadnesses which had been well brushed away from my heart since my advent to this place. I must admit that in experiencing the immortality of being, I found that I experienced no less the immortality of love.

Had I to meet that old conflict *here*? I never asked for everlasting life. Will He impose it, and not free me from *that*? God forgive me! Have I evil in my heart still? Can one sin in Heaven? Nay, be merciful, be merciful! I will be patient. I will have trust. But the old nerves are not dead. The old ache has survived the grave.

Why was this permitted, if without a cure? Why had death no power to call decay upon that for which eternal life seemed to have provided no health? It had seemed to me, so far as I could observe the heavenly society, that only the fortunate affections of preëxistence survived. The unhappy, as well as the imperfect, were outlived and replaced. Mysteries had presented themselves here, which I was not yet wise enough to clear up. I saw, however, that a great ideal was one thing which never died. The attempt to realize it often involved effects which seemed hardly less than miraculous.

But for myself, events had brought no solution of the problems of my past; and with the tenacity of a constant nature I was unable to see any for the future.

I mused one evening, alone with these long thoughts. I was strolling upon a wide, bright field. Behind me lay the city, glittering and glad. Beyond, I saw the little sea which I had crossed. The familiar outline of the hills uprose behind. All Heaven seemed heavenly. I heard distant merry voices and music. Listening closely, I found that the Wedding March that had stirred so many human heart-beats was perfectly performed somewhere across the water, and that the wind bore the sounds towards me. I then remembered to have heard it said that Mendelssohn was himself a guest of some distinguished person in an adjacent town, and that certain music of his was to be given for the entertainment of a group of people who had been deaf-mutes in the lower life.

As the immortal power of the old music filled the air, I stayed my steps to listen. The better to do this, I covered my eyes with my hands, and so stood blindfold and alone in the midst of the wide field.

The passion of earth and the purity of Heaven—the passion of Heaven and the deferred hope of earth—what loss and what possession were in the throbbing strains!

As never on earth, they called the glad to rapture. As never on earth, they stirred the sad to silence. Where, before, had soul or sense been called by such a clarion? What music was, we used to dream. What it is, we dare, at last, to know.

And yet—I would have been spared this if I could, I think, just now. Give me a moment's grace. I would draw breath, and so move on again, and turn me to my next duty quietly, since even Heaven denies me, after all.

I would—what would I? Where am I? Who spoke, or stirred? WHO called me by a name unheard by me of any living lip for almost twenty years?

In a transport of something not unlike terror, I could not remove my hands from my eyes, but still stood, blinded and dumb, in the middle of the shining field. Beneath my clasped fingers, I caught the radiance of the edges of the blades of grass that the low breeze swept against my garment's hem; and strangely in that strange moment, there came to me, for the only articulate thought I could command, these two lines of an old hymn:

"Sweet fields beyond the swelling flood
Stand dressed in living green."

"Take down your hands," a voice said quietly. "Do not start or fear. It is the most natural thing in the world that I should find you. Be calm. Take courage. Look at me."

Obeying, as the tide obeys the moon, I gathered heart, and so, lifting my eyes, I saw him whom I remembered standing close beside me. We two were alone in the wide, bright field. All Heaven seemed to have withdrawn to leave us to ourselves for this one moment.

I had known that I might have loved him, all my life. I had never loved any other man. I had not seen him for almost twenty years. As our eyes met, our souls challenged one another in silence, and in strength. I was the first to speak:

"*Where is she?*"

"Not with me."

"When did you die?"

"Years ago."

"I had lost all trace of you."

"It was better so, for all concerned."

"Is she—is she"—

"She is on earth, and of it; she has found comfort long since; another fills my place. I do not grieve to yield it. Come!"

"But I have thought—for all these years—it was not right—I put the thought away—I do not understand"—

"Oh, come! I, too, have waited twenty years."

"But is there no reason—no barrier—are you sure? God help me! You have turned Heaven into Hell for me, if this is not right."

"Did I ever ask you to give me one pitying thought that was not right?"

"Never, God knows. Never. You helped me to be right, to be noble. You were the noblest man I ever knew. I was a better woman for having known you, though we parted—as we did."

"Then do you trust me? Come!"

"I trust you as I do the angels of God."

"And I love you as His angels may. Come!"

"For how long—am I to come?"

"Are we not in Eternity? I claim you as I have loved you, without limit and without end. Soul of my immortal soul! Life of my eternal life!—Ah, come."

XV.

AND yet so subtle is the connection in the eternal life between the soul's best moments and the Source of them, that I felt unready for my joy until it had His blessing whose Love was the sun of all love, and whose approval was sweeter than all happiness.

Now, it was a part of that beautiful order of Heaven, which we ceased to call accident, that while I had this wish upon my lips, we saw Him coming to us, where we still stood alone together in the open field.

We did not hasten to meet Him, but remained as we were until He reached our side; and then we sank upon our knees before Him, silently. God knows what gain we had for the life that we had lost below. The pure eyes of the Master sought us with a benignity from which we thanked the Infinite Mercy that our own had not need to droop ashamed. What weak, earthly comfort could have been worth the loss of a moment such as this? He blesses us. With His sacred hands He blesses us, and by His blessing lifts our human love into so divine a thing that this seems the only life in which it could have breathed.

By-and-by, when our Lord has left us, we join hands like children, and walk quietly through the dazzling air, across the field, and up the hill, and up the road, and home. I seek my mother, trembling, and clasp her, sinking on my knees, until I hide my face upon her lap. Her hands stray across my hair and cheek.

"What is the matter, Mary?—*dear* Mary!"

"Oh, Mother, I have Heaven in my heart at last!"

"Tell me all about it, my poor child. Hush! There, there! my dear!"

"*Your poor child?* ... Mother! What *can* you mean?"—

What can she mean, indeed? I turn and gaze into her eyes. My face was hidden in her lap. Her hands stray across my hair and cheek.

"*What is the matter, Mary?—dear Mary!*"

"*Oh, Mother, I have Heaven in my heart at last!*"

"*Tell me all about it, my poor child. Hush! There, there! my dear!*"

"*Your poor child? Mother! What* CAN *this mean?*"

She broods and blesses me, she calms and gathers me. With a mighty cry, I fling myself against her heart, and sob my soul out, there.

"You are better, child," she says. "Be quiet. You will live."

Upon the edge of the sick-bed, sitting strained and weary, she leans to comfort me. The night-lamp burns dimly on the floor behind the door. The great red chair stands with my white woollen wrapper thrown across the arm. In the window the magenta geranium droops freezing. Mignonette is on the table, and its breath pervades the air. Upon the wall, the cross, the Christ, and the picture of my father look down.

The doctor is in the room; I hear him say that he shall change the medicine, and some one, I do not notice who, whispers that it is thirty hours since the stupor, from which I have aroused, began. Alice comes in, and Tom, I see, has taken Mother's place, and holds me—dear Tom!—and asks me if I suffer, and why I look so disappointed.

Without, in the frosty morning, the factory-bells are calling the poor girls to their work. The shutter is ajar, and through the crack I see the winter day dawn on the world.

CPSIA information can be obtained
at www.ICGtesting.com
Printed in the USA
LVHW110457240821
695968LV00005B/336